Promises

Book One of The Syrenka Series

Amber Garr

Promises

Book One of The Syrenka Series

by Amber Garr

Copyright © 2011 Amber Garr

www.ambergarr.com

This is a work of fiction. The names, characters, places, and incidents are products of the author's imagination or have been used fictitiously and are not to be construed as real. Any resemblance to actual persons, living or dead, events, or locales is entirely coincidental.

All rights are reserved. No part of this book may be used or reproduced in any manner whatsoever without written permission from the author.

Cover Design by PhatPuppyArt

ISBN-13: 978-1468006797
ISBN-10: 1468006797

ACKNOWLEDGEMENTS

I would most graciously like to thank my group of beta readers who have taken time out of their busy lives to help make this book possible. To my mom, Sandy, Elizabeth, Jocelyn, and Erin…I can never thank you enough for your encouragement. This is something that means a lot to me and I am so glad that you have been a part of this process. And also thanks to my friends and coworkers who have been tremendously supportive of my endeavor.

ONE

I barely heard her parting words as the screen door slammed shut. My head spun in desperation as the anger coursed through my bones. "Get back in here Eviana!" she continued to scream at me. "We are not finished with this conversation!"

I was already racing down the deck stairs toward the sandy beach, kicking off my shoes and unbuttoning my blouse. *We are for now*, I thought as my blood boiled with rage and resentment. I was going to be trapped! How dare they? This was not the eighteenth century anymore! I had *rights*!

I stumbled onto the sand, taking just a brief moment to savor the warmth and the feeling of the grains massaging my toes. My shirt came off and I started to unzip my jeans. No one was around. But I wouldn't care anyway. The water was calling me and it was the only voice that I could hear now. With one pant leg off, I hopped along in my forward progression until the other one was free. My oasis was so close now that I could taste the salt in the air. The sun broke free of a cloud, stopping me for a moment. It was late afternoon with sunset still a few hours away, but the sky had already turning multiple shades of pink and orange. The coloration reminded me of the inside of a brilliant conch shell.

I closed my eyes and took a deep breath. I knew there would be hell to pay when I returned to the house. Marguerite, my mother, had tolerated my rebellious behavior when I was younger, giving me more freedom and second chances than anyone in our clan. But apparently now, at seventeen, I was an adult. Adult enough to bear children. Adult enough to participate in clan gatherings. Adult enough to navigate our youth through their transition period. But *not* adult enough to choose who to love.

A slight breeze wafted off the ocean, bringing with it scents that filled my gut with longing. The freedom of the ocean. Why couldn't I just stay there forever? A gull called overhead, beckoning me to join him. The splashing waves calmed my inner rage as they ebbed and flowed in a hypnotic pattern. A distant moan of a shipping vessel reminded me of our history. I opened my eyes to see that I was standing alone along miles of sandy beach interlaced with large rocks and cliffs emblematic of the northern California coast. So beautiful. I stripped off the rest of my clothes and ran into the ocean.

As soon as I was under the water, I could feel the transition begin. My lower body ached as the bones adjusted from a life on land to one at sea. Both legs began to fuse together and work as one. My foot bones elongated while I prepared for the agony. I was accustomed to the changes now, but it was still a struggle of mind over matter. Breaking through the surface of the water, I grabbed one last breath before the final jolt of pain ravaged through my body. I bit my bottom lip and squeezed my eyes shut, willing the moment to be over. At last I felt an electric tingle move from my hips to my toes as the hardened iridescent, scales appeared on my tail. I opened my eyes to find that the internal transformation was complete as well. My vision cleared. My lungs expanded. I could hear for miles. I was free.

So I swam. I swam away from the shore and the house that I lived in. I swam away from my fears and obligations as though they could disappear with the distance. I would temporarily forget my responsibilities, my duties, and the argument with my mother. In here, I wasn't trapped. The sea was my true home. I was a mermaid and this was my world.

The sun pushed through the water, highlighting the kelp and creating a kaleidoscope of light beams piercing the blue depths of the ocean. Gathering up all of the negative energy, I smiled and thrust that power into my movement. I darted over and under and around the light beams, challenging myself not to hit any of the massive algal trees. I chased the fish and raced with the sea otters, laughing as they tried to decide if I was friend or foe.

My hair flowed behind me like a golden cape while I dove to the sea floor and skimmed over the bottom like a fighter jet. In a daring move that most of my clan members would find disgraceful and childish, I pumped my tail and hurdled toward the surface. As I broke free from the water, I caught a glimpse of the shoreline miles away where my house was barely visible. Flying through the air like a circus performer, I gathered my breath just before diving to the ocean depths once again.

My body relaxed as I slipped into a more peaceful swimming pattern and let my mind drift away. I didn't need to speak. I didn't need to listen. I just *was*. I turned back toward the shore but began to move diagonally to the north. I knew this section of water well. Every rock outcropping, kelp bed, and reef was a marker on the map in my labyrinth of a mind. The ocean was calm today, allowing me to see nearly a hundred feet around. I stayed close to the bottom, rising and falling over the contours of the seascape.

I was almost to my destination when a shadow darted over my head. It caused me to stop and spin around so fast that my hair tangled in my face. As I struggled to move it away from my eyes, I tried to sense if something was around me. Although mermaids were pretty much at the top of the food chain in this part of the ocean, our natural animal instincts were hard to suppress.

I closed my eyes and tried to listen for movement or feel for the electrical pulses all living creatures exude. Nothing. My hair was so wrapped up around my face that I kept my eyes closed and used both hands to separate the knotted mess. Finally, I broke free from my temporary imprisonment and when I opened my eyes, a large seal was staring at me.

While trying to stifle a scream, he looked into my eyes, cocked his head slightly, and blew a rush of bubbles into my face. I grabbed for him with both arms, trying to capture his massive body, but instead my hands barely grazed his tail flippers. He slipped past me and rushed to the surface. I raced after him while we both grabbed a quick breath, thinking that this was my chance to slow him down. But he was too quick, and before I could get my head back under the water, I felt a jolt against my stomach as he tried to toss me into the air.

He failed and I was able to make a quick snatch of his side flipper that yanked him back toward me. We twisted and turned and jockeyed around each other, trying to get the upper hand. When we would get close to crashing into the sea floor, we'd change direction and struggle back toward the surface. It must have looked like a bubble torpedo oscillating through the vast emptiness with no target in its sites.

I suddenly pulled free from the seal and took off as fast as I could toward the nearest kelp bed. He was too quick and managed to nip my tail just as I flitted into the great forest. We dodged and dived between the leaves. I was fast, but he was more agile with his sleek body shape.

Sensing my imminent defeat, I tried one last maneuver. Wrapping my hands around the largest trunk of algae I could find, I used all of the strength in my arms to swing my body around behind it. The movement caught him by surprise and he was swimming too fast to correct for it. The seal sailed past me but before he could turn around, I bounded out with one powerful kick. Jetting over him, I encircled my arms around his neck and maneuvered my body over his back. He flipped around several times trying to knock me free, but I had him.

I felt a laugh rumble through his body as he slowed to a casual swimming pace, ultimately conceding defeat. Smiling, I nestled my face against his neck as he carried me away.

We came to a small rock island a few miles offshore. On the west side, a tiny gravel littered cove was nestled in between two high cliffs, effectively blocking the view to the east. The setting sun cast shards of orange, red, and purple against the volcanic sheets of rock like a giant gothic crystal prism. This side of the island was hidden from the shore. This side of the island was our sanctuary.

I let go of my furry chariot and sat in the shallows while concentrating on my transition. Turning back into human form was always easier for me and in just a few moments I was walking on two legs again. I watched the seal hurl himself out of the water and onto the rocky shore. He glanced my way, snorted, and turned his back to me. In a move so graceful it could only be magical, the seal pushed back onto his hind flippers…and became a human.

The fur coat fell from his body as he took a deep breath; his face upwards toward the cliff. Even from behind, he was breathtaking. We've known each other since we were kids and every time I saw him my heart jumped and my stomach fluttered. I started to move toward him, oblivious of my nakedness and captivated by his. It wasn't an issue in our world and especially not at our sanctuary. The human body was just a part of who we were. He turned his head slightly and sighed, but I could see the smile from where I was.

"I thought that we weren't going to meet until tomorrow." He shook his head. "You caught me off guard and bested me."

I was about to argue that he had surprised me too, but when he turned around to face me I froze. His tall, athletic build was just a fraction of what made me catch my breath. The tanned skin and dark hair complimented the sharp angles on his face and enhanced the mesmerizing green of his eyes. Since the first day I met him, he could overwhelm me with his smile. It was one of his best features. However, it was the way he looked at *me* that had captured my heart so many years ago. His laugh snapped me out of my temporary paralysis.

"Have I bewildered you again, my sexy siren?"

I smiled and closed the distance between us before he could speak again. We kissed for several minutes, exploring every surface of our human forms.

I lost myself in him until reality came crashing back, knocking the breath away from me. I pulled away so suddenly, I almost tripped over my feet. Tears filled my eyes.

"Eviana. What is it? What's wrong?" He bent down toward me placing both hands on my arms to hold me up.

"They did it Brendan! They have made the arrangements, and there's nothing I can do about it!" I didn't want to scream at him, but all of the emotion I'd pushed aside during our swim came flooding back. I hated them right now. "How could they do this to us?" I pleaded and slammed my arms down against my legs. "They have no *right!*"

Brendan's hands caressed my arms and then he pulled me in to his chest where I could burrow in his warmth. He sighed, kissed the top of my head, and rested his chin there for a while.

A few moments passed before he calmly and stoically replied, "We knew that this day would come sometime. Now we will have to figure out what we are going to do about it."

"What we're going to do about it? *What we're going to do about it?* We're going to run away from this place. So far away that they will never come after us. I will not live without you and I will *not* marry Kain!"

"You can't leave your clan Evs. Perhaps we could talk to them…"

"*Talk?*" I replied, sounding very immature as I cut him off. "Don't you think I already tried that? Marguerite will not listen to me. She doesn't care about my feelings. "*It is your duty Eviana. You will marry Kain and breed for the good of the clan*"," I imitated in a not-so-good impression of our leader.

There were not many merfolk left in the world; therefore each clan would purposely arrange marriages and partnerships in order to keep the bloodline strong and healthy. Kain and I had been promised to each other since we were children. He grew up on the northern east coast, so I would only see him once a year during our gatherings. As we got older, he would visit California more often, being sure to partake in our clan's hospitality each time.

In all fairness, he would not have been a bad choice for someone. He was attractive, funny, and had been in love with me since we were five. He came from a line of leaders and always presented himself as such. Despite my subtle and palpable attempts to encourage him to find someone else, he never seemed to be interested in other girls. And my heart had always belonged to another.

Brendan and I met when I was ten, during one of my clan's trips to Seattle. I had just experienced my first transition and was still learning how to control my urges not to live permanently in the sea. Therefore I was a bit…moody. During the first few years, a young mermaid lives many lifetimes over while trying to manage the changes, the perils of puberty, and creating excuses for your friends as to why you can't go to the beach with them anymore.

My first years were hell. On this particular trip, I was behaving badly and Marguerite sent me out of the house "until I knew what I was sorry for". So, undoubtedly, my walk lasted for hours. I'd finally found a path and climbed down to the rocky beach, sprawling over top of a large boulder. At some point I must have fallen asleep to the rhythmic sounds of the ocean, because when I woke up, I was smothered by a seal as large as me. His strange green eyes hovered above mine and he made no attempt to move away.

He weighed so much I couldn't push him off, yet I could still throw a punch. Hitting him right in the snout, I felt a wave of satisfaction as I heard a whelp escape the pup. He recovered quickly. So quickly, in fact, that before I knew what was happening, he'd grabbed my leg in his mouth and pulled me into the water with him.

For a few brief moments I panicked. Not because I was under the water, but because I could already feel my bones begin to ache. While dealing with the terror of my impending transition and trying to disrobe underwater (which is not an easy task), that wretched little seal kept darting over me. He would slam into my shoulders, push against my back, and then swim in a circle around me so that I was trapped in the swirl of his wake.

But the moment I got my clothes off, he stopped.

Intent on not being an embarrassed, naked, prepubescent girl, I sunk deeper under the water and stubbornly turned to face him. I focused on his eyes as I felt my legs fuse and the scales appear, while trying to hide all traces of my mental discomfort and physical anguish.

His reaction appeared to be humanlike, and I swear I caught him staring at my breasts. As he began to slink closer, I held my ground. When he swam around examining me like a freak show exhibit, I remained still. It wasn't until the moment that he circled back to my face that I struck. Grabbing his neck and swinging my tail behind him, I wrapped my arms around his body and dug my hands into his blubbery folds. Just as I got a decent grip, he took off.

With my new tail, I was actually longer than him but he was much faster. We swam around for miles, jostling for the better position but never letting go of each other. When it was time for a rest, he took me to a secluded beach where we changed and talked for hours. We discovered what type of creatures we both were, learning that we had more in common than any of our friends could possibly understand.

Brendan was a selkie. A shapeshifter of sorts, like me, but belonging to a totally different line of them. His transitions occurred when he placed the seal skin on his body and became one with it. Although he claimed that he didn't feel quite the same intense call to the ocean as me, he did admit that he needed to shift on a regular basis or risk getting sick. That's why he'd been in the sea that day. It had been too long since his last transformation and he was feeling weak.

Brendan's father lived in the Pacific Northwest, and although he was only three years older than me, he would be left to fend for himself in another couple of years. When I tried to understand why he would leave his home so young, he moved on to questions about me and my family.

That beach became our world for a few hours. And that world contained just the two of us. My earlier acts of disobedience had led me to my first selkie, my first kiss, and my only true love.

Over the next several years, we wrote letters, sent emails, talked on the phone, and made plans about our future together. When our families were visiting nearby, we'd arrange to sneak out and spend hours together. Sometimes we would swim. Sometimes we would just lay in the sun and talk.

Our lives molded together so perfectly that we tried to forget about our birthrights and duties and pretend that we could make this work. I wasn't the only one promised to a life of breeding. Selkie men are required to seduce and impregnate human females since their species cannot reproduce amongst themselves. It was a life Brendan despised.

But the merfolk are different. We are incapable of breeding with humans, and therefore, are trapped in arranged marriages and intolerable obligations. This was a burden I had never wanted to bear.

"Puh-lease. Your mother doesn't sound anything like that." Brendan's attempt at humor brought me back to the present.

I tried to smile at him, but the grin barely touched the corners of my mouth. "Yes she does." I pulled away from him to look into his beautiful green eyes. "What are we going to do?" I could hardly control the tears threatening to burst their dam.

"You will return to your home and family and..." he placed a finger over my lips when I started to protest. "And we will pretend that we've accepted our fate. We will continue living our lives as though we are content." He arched an eyebrow and smirked. "Well, you will continue to act as you normally do and harass everyone to death." Before I could take a bite of his finger in response to his jab, he quickly moved it away from my lips.

"And then what?" I asked indignantly.

"And then in one month, we leave." He was so sure. So secure in this declaration that it took me a few seconds to believe what I was hearing.

"Really?" I pleaded, this time allowing more excitement to filter into my question. "Please tell me you mean this."

"I will not live without you Eviana. I cannot."

I launched myself into his arms and wrapped my legs around his waist kissing him at the same time. "I love you Brendan, but please promise me that you will go."

He hugged me close and whispered into my ear, "I promise."

Two

My swim home was too quick. Lost in the elation of Brendan's promise, I thought about what I could take with me when I left my home. Maybe one suitcase and my iPod; we could always replace what we couldn't carry. Would we fly or drive? Where would we go? Brendan had promised to make all of the necessary arrangements soon, but I didn't know if I could wait to hear his plan.

Night was nearly here and the silhouette of my house looked bleak and menacing. When I reached our backyard stretch of beach, someone was waiting for me. I sighed and picked up my scattered clothing without acknowledging my guest.

"You are in so much trouble this time," a whiney, nasally voice taunted.

"Shut up, Marisol and mind your own business." I walked briskly back to the stairs, trying to ignore my sister, but she followed closely at my heels.

"I don't understand what's wrong with you. This is what we were born to do and Kain is super rich and totally gorgeous." She tripped on one of the steps and stumbled into me. I turned with a glare so evil that she stepped away. "He doesn't deserve you."

The words were sharp but I knew that they rang true. Kain didn't deserve someone who couldn't love him. He was too good and too nice. My sister was right, but that didn't mean I had to let her know it.

"You don't even know what you're talking about *Mars*," I snapped at her, using the childhood nickname she loathed. "Just mind your own business for once and leave me alone!"

Stomping up the stairs was probably a mistake. Although I managed to lose one nagging voice, two more were waiting for me at the top. I looked into my parents eyes and could see their growing disappointment. The dark wood deck wrapped entirely around the raised first floor of our house and was large enough to hold a hundred people. But there were only two of them standing there now. They leaned against the railing on the far side with my father holding my mother in front of him in a show of support and unity. I rolled my eyes.

"Told you," chirped Marisol as she dodged out of the way of my swinging hand.

"Eviana Anne Dumahl. Do not strike your sister." My father's harsh command sent chills through my body. I really hated it when he was this mad at me. "And put some clothes on."

I was standing before them completely naked and soaking wet. Succumbing to the grueling glares, I reluctantly pulled on my blouse using my arms to secure it to my body rather than button it up.

"Where did you go?" my father asked in a lighter tone.

Before I could answer, my mother cut in, "You were with *him* weren't you?" She pulled away from my father's arms and walked toward me with determination. Her long dark hair flowed around her perfectly smooth face. The grace and confidence with which she moved still astounded me.

Without looking into her eyes, I threw back my shoulders and stood my ground. Anything to defy her.

She literally sniffed me. Her nose moved around my neck, my hair, and even my hands. There was no way that I could deny who I'd spent the last few hours with, and I wouldn't try to anyway.

"I want to be with him. Not Kain."

My mother tsked at me in disgust and grabbed my face with her hands. She was slightly shorter than me, but her domineering personality was still intimidating. Plus she was squeezing my cheeks pretty hard.

"You will not see that boy again, do you understand? The Matthews have finally agreed to conduct this marriage and you will respect your duties and your family. This is very important to our survival. Can you even begin to comprehend what type of message your behavior is sending?"

I could see the frustration building in her eyes, and before I realized what was happening, my tears spilled over. I pushed her hands away and turned to my father.

"Please, dad. Please! Don't make me do this!" I waved my arm back toward the house. "Marisol would kill to have the chance to marry Kain and provide him children. Why can't she just do it?"

"Oh Eviana, please don't upset yourself like this." He glided over and wrapped me in an embrace. His warm body and soothing voice kept offering false hope.

"Stop babying her, Charles," my mother snapped. "She is almost eighteen now. It's about time she started acting like it."

Marguerite, my mother and the Dumahl Clan leader, didn't stop there. "You and I had to endure our marriage when we were much younger than this." Turning toward me, she continued, "I became a leader when I was your age. I survived. Charles and I survived. And so will you. Stop acting like a spoiled brat and accept your responsibility!"

My mother walked away toward the deck's edge to regain her composure and my father sighed. I knew what was coming next.

"Eviana, you must do as you are told. Kain is a nice young man with a good family. And from what I can see, he is already quite smitten with you."

I sobbed out of control. I really did hate to disappoint my father and even my mother sometimes. But this is not the life I wanted. I suddenly realized that I wasn't crying because I'd have to marry Kain, I was crying because I knew that I had to run away. There was no other choice at this point.

Feigning total defeat, I pulled away and looked up at him. His middle-aged face could pass for someone ten years younger, but the wrinkles around his eyes did little to hide his distress. I'd probably been the cause of most of those lines.

"When is it?" I asked.

Both of my parents looked at me in shock. They shared a glance between them, no doubt trying to figure out if this was a trick. My mother replied hesitantly, "The first of the month."

"What? But that's in less than two weeks! I won't even be eighteen yet." And Brendan and I won't have a chance to leave.

"You don't have to be eighteen. We are giving our permission," my father said with a questioning tone.

"But…can't we postpone it until after my birthday? That's only another couple of days. I'm sure Kain wouldn't mind."

"It's already been arranged, Eviana. Stop being so difficult," my mother said while wrapping her arms around my father's waist.

He looked down at her. "Marguerite, I imagine we could wait a few more days. The Matthews would be amenable."

"You spoil her, Charles. This is why she acts the way she does." She sighed dramatically and thought about his request. Her lips pursed together and she stared intensely at me for a full minute. "Fine. I'll talk to them. But you will be married the weekend after your birthday. That gives you plenty of time to say goodbye to that selkie boy."

My gut twitched with a mixture of relief, anger, and anticipation. I'd just bought myself a few extra days, and although I hated my mother's attitude toward him, I knew that Brendan and I would be gone by that time.

"Thank you," I said somberly. "I won't disappoint you." My mother huffed and my dad smiled. I turned to walk into the house when they called my attention back to them.

"There's something else." Her voice was clipped with the business tone and I knew that I wasn't going to like whatever it was that she planned to say. "We are sending you to The Cotillion this year. You leave tomorrow."

"What? Why?" The Cotillion was an annual gathering of the merfolk *syrenka*, or the apprentice adults. Once we reached marriage age, which was anywhere from sixteen to twenty, the guardians would prepare and train us for our future in clan politics. Likewise, if someone wasn't already promised in marriage, The Cotillion served as a sort of matchmaking ball.

My mother continued, "Since you will be marrying Kain, you both will be attending this year. His father is not aging well, and Kain is the next in line for leadership. You will present yourself as a couple and Harlan will serve as your guardian."

Harlan Matthew was Kain's father and leader of their clan. I'd only met him a couple of times, so I didn't know how the next few days would go. Kain and I got along well enough, but it was never a completely comfortable situation.

"But what about school?"

"The arrangements have been made." I think that was my mother's favorite phrase.

"Well, when do I leave?"

"Tomorrow evening," my father said calmly and then smiled. "I think you'll like the location."

"Yeah?"

"Yes. You are going to Florida. Well, the Florida Keys to be more specific. The Donnellys are hosting this year."

Florida didn't sound like that bad of an idea, although I really wished Brendan could go with me instead. I'd never been there and apparently the Donnellys were one of the wealthiest clans next to the Matthews and the Dumahls. Rumor had it that they owned their own island.

"Enough for now," my mother cut in. "Go inside, shower, and pack for tomorrow. I'll get your travel documents ready." She stepped closer to me, put her hands on my shoulders, and stared into my eyes. "I expect you to be on your best behavior Eviana Dumahl. If I so much as hear *one* negative comment from anyone, and I mean anyone, you will be locked in this house until I can marry you off to the Matthews. Do you understand me?"

I swallowed hard, fighting my urge to respond. My father caught my glance and pleaded with his eyes until I reluctantly nodded my head.

"Good," she breathed. "Now get inside."

I turned to cross the rest of the deck, but not before stripping off my blouse and sashaying away in all of my naked glory. There is always a way to get the last word.

Once inside, I immediately went up the stairs toward my third floor bedroom. Our house was ridiculously large with eight bedrooms and nine bathrooms plus a guest cottage over the garage. The beach location was prime and many years ago, our ancestors purchased multiple tracks of land to allow for the privacy our kind desires. We all went to elite private schools, all had new cars as soon as we could drive, and wanted for nothing. I guess that was part of the tradeoff for being forced to marry and mate once you became an adult. They stole your freedom later in life therefore they spoiled you rotten early on.

"So, did they rip you a new one?" Marisol's high-pitched annoying voice ripped me from my thoughts. "Are you permanently grounded for the next two weeks?" She was standing in the hall, blocking the path to my door.

"Get out of my way," I threatened.

Ignoring me, she stepped closer and stood on her tip toes to get right in my face. "You are a disgrace to this family. I can't wait until you leave with the Matthews."

I envisioned how good it would feel to punch her and watch as her bloody nose clogged her piercing voice, but instead of acting, I took a deep breath. The best way to handle Marisol was to not take the bait. So I stood and waited for her to give up.

"Not going to fight me, huh? My, my…they must have really punished you this time." She swayed from side to side, trying to encourage a reaction. Believe me, it was hard to restrain myself. Finally, she sighed and blew a cloud of hot air in my face. "Whatever," she huffed and walked away.

I stood there for another moment wondering if I would miss her when Brendan and I left. My father, yes. My mother…probably. But Marisol, I don't think so. She had a mean streak in her ten times worse than my mother's. In all honestly, she would make for a much better leader than me. Her cold, detached personality would serve her well in that capacity. And when I left, she would be next in line. Although she was only fourteen, perhaps they would send her to Cotillion next year and marry her off to Kain. It would be her dream come true.

For the next hour, I packed all of the cute sundresses, wedges, and jewelry I could fit into my suitcase. I did manage to squeeze in my one ball gown that we purchased last year at my mother's insistence. It had never been worn, and I was secretly excited to finally try it out, even though I would never let my mother know.

After my shower, I tried to call Brendan. He didn't answer, but when I realized what time it was, I knew the reason. He had just turned twenty-one and was now a full bartender at one of the beach bars in the next town over. It was a little dive, but during the peak season, it was packed with tourists and an eclectic group of locals. At least that's what he had told me, I've never been there.

I envied Brendan for his work ethic and drive. He was forced to leave home at sixteen and managed to graduate from college last year with a biology degree while working every night at one job or another. His maturity far surpassed mine, and I often wondered why he wanted to put up with me. I was spoiled and pampered and never really had a goal other than to not marry Kain and not have his children.

Opening my journal, I jotted down three words: *Find a purpose.* Since I had a long flight and even longer weekend ahead of me, I vowed to make Brendan proud of me by maturing. As I smiled to myself in pride, my phone beeped with a text message.

Sorry. Busy tonight. Everything OK? It was Brendan.

I replied instantly. *Yes. No. They are sending me to Cotillion tomorrow night. In Florida! Meet after school?*

It was another minute before he responded. *Absolutely. See you at the point.* That was our second favorite private spot, and it wasn't as far away as our island.

OK. Be there by 4. Miss you. Love you.

Love you too Evs. Sweet dreams.

I wanted to run to the bar and wrap my arms around him now. The only thing keeping me in bed was my vision of what our life was going to be like together. No one telling us that we can't date. No one telling us what to eat or drink. No one making plans about our future. It would be wonderful.

I fell asleep with a smile on my face dreaming about our first apartment together and counting down the days until my escape.

THREE

The school day was one of the slowest ones ever. It was a Thursday, which meant extra long classes but fewer of them. I managed to talk with a couple of my girlfriends at lunch which only made things worse. Apparently Justin Bernard was having a major party this weekend and that was all anyone could talk about. Justin was a senior and the coolest guy in school. Cute, athletic, rich, human…enough said. He'd actually invited a few of my friends personally and it had made their entire week.

Unfortunately, I was not going to be able to go and when I thought about the reason why, it just depressed me more. When the final bell rang, I checked my watch to see that I had thirty minutes to get to our meeting spot. Brendan usually slept during the day due to his night schedule, but I would imagine that he'd still beat me there.

I fumbled with my bag that kept slipping off my shoulder, so I wasn't paying attention to my surroundings. When I got to the end of the pathway and raised my head, my heart dropped. Sitting in front of me, waiting for the end of the school day, was a sleek white limousine with tinted windows and a distinctive blue wave emblem on the side door. I sighed and swore under my breath.

The driver's side door opened, and a tall man in a black chauffeur suit stepped out. He nodded his head at me and waved toward the back door. "Miss Dumahl."

"Hi Jeffery." I moved a little closer and bent down to try and see inside. "Why are you here?" Maybe my suspicions were wrong.

"I am taking you and Mr. Matthew to the airport. Didn't your mother tell you?"

I knew it. This had probably been her plan all along. "No, she didn't. I wasn't supposed to leave until later tonight."

Jeffery looked perplexed and said, "Well, there must have been some kind of miscommunication. Your flights are in just over an hour, so we need to go to the airport now. Mistress Dumahl gave me your belongings and I've already collected Mr. Matthew."

"Kain's in there?" I squinted my eyes in an attempt to see through the tint. My heart fluttered slightly knowing that our weekend was already beginning. But more importantly, I felt nervous because I was going to have to talk to Brendan in front of him.

"Miss Dumahl. Please." Jeffery ushered me to the back door which he promptly opened and encouraged me inside. A blast of chilled air hit me like a wall and I instantly tightened the sweater around me. The leather seat squeaked when I sat down and the smell of the sea mixed with a hint of cologne overpowered my senses.

"Hey Eviana," a warm, smooth voice greeted me. I turned to see Kain's beautiful smiling face. The baby blue eyes paired nicely with his light blonde hair. It was longer now, and hung around his face and ears. He wore a pair of jeans and a black sweater with a white collared shirt peeking out from underneath. In simple terms, he looked good as always.

Kain removed his sunglasses and flipped them around a few times in his hand, seemingly anxious to see what my attitude would be today. It was a nervous habit of his, he always had to have something moving in his hands. I couldn't help but smile.

"Hi Kain. What are you doing here?" Although he split his time between Los Angeles and Boston, he usually stayed on the east coast. And if he was in town, my parents made sure that he stopped by our house.

He smiled. "My dad had business in L.A. and he wanted me to tag along. We drove up here this morning." Yes, apparently so the parents could arrange a marriage behind our backs.

"And now they're shipping us off to Florida for a fun-filled weekend," I said with more than a hint of sarcasm.

"Not so thrilled to go, are you?" He laughed at my discomfort. "It might be kind of fun, don't you think? I mean, we've never been to Florida before and the water is actually warm. Plus, they have lots of dolphins!"

"We have dolphins too," I countered.

"Porpoise. And how many times do you actually see them here? I think the sharks scare them away."

I rolled my eyes at him in response. Jeffery began driving away from the school to the awaiting airport. The weekend had begun and my heart ached as I thought about Brendan.

"So, did they tell you where we're staying?" Kain continued.

"Nope. All I know is that the Donnellys are hosting this year. My parents didn't even tell me about this until last night."

"Well, that's because they hadn't settled on a date yet..." his words trailed off, realizing that he'd just brought up the subject of our impending marriage.

"So where are we staying?" I asked trying to break the tension.

"Oh, with Master Donnelly himself. Actually, I think they gave us the boat house. We'll be so close to the water." His eyes were filled with excitement and hope. I wasn't sure if it was the tranquil Florida seas or my presence as his betrothed that had him so elated. Time for a quick subject change.

"How's your dad doing?" I asked.

His smile faltered and he sank back into the seat. "Okay, I guess. Some days are good, some are bad. He's going to meet us there tomorrow morning. I think there were some things he and your mom had to discuss without us being around."

"I'm sure there were," I groaned. My mother completely planned this. Not only did her little stunt force Kain and me to travel together as a couple, but she had the opportunity to finalize the wedding plans while I was out of the state. I was reminded of another meeting and pulled out my phone. Kain shifted in his seat and stared at me with a look that made my stomach drop.

"I'm sorry, but I need to call Brendan." I could see the excitement fall from his face and disappointment settle in instead. "We were supposed to meet after school, so I need to let him know what's going on."

Kain shook his head a little too ambitiously in an attempt to feign understanding. "Yeah, sure. Go ahead." He put his sunglasses back on and looked out the window.

I felt really uncomfortable making this call in front of someone who had feelings for me, but my mother gave me no other option. The phone rang three times before he answered.

"Evs? Where are you?"

"On my way to the airport," I sighed.

"What? Oh, wait, let me guess…your mother?"

"Bingo. Totally planned, I'm sure. She even arranged to get Kain here." I turned to look at him when I mentioned his name, but he continued to stare out the window. "We leave in an hour, and it will probably be late by the time we get there. I'll let you know though."

"When do you get back?"

"Monday, sometime."

"Okay, we can get together the night you get home. Let me know when you're back and I'll tell you where." I smiled and my heart fluttered. I could always trust Brendan to come through with a plan.

"Thanks," I said wholeheartedly.

"For what?"

"For being you. I love you." I tried to peek over toward Kain again, lowering my voice so that he wouldn't have to hear so much. It was pointless though, and I saw his head drop.

"Love you too. Have a safe flight and try to enjoy yourself. I'll be here when you get back." He was so confident and sweet that I couldn't stop my eyes from tearing up. I hated to spend more than a day away from him.

We hung up and I pulled my sunglasses back down to cover my sorrow. The car turned onto the highway, reminding me that we were getting closer to the airport. Kain and I didn't speak for several minutes until he brought up a subject that I was hoping to avoid.

"Did you tell him?" I knew he was referring to the marriage and I rolled my head against the seat to look at him. He was nervous but sincere in his question. My relationship with Brendan had never been hidden or off limits, even though Kain was the last person I wanted to discuss it with.

"Yes, last night." I didn't elaborate and after a few moments he continued.

"I know that you don't want to marry me," he shook his head when I opened my mouth to say something. "But it looks like we don't have much of a choice. I'm glad that I get to spend this weekend with you because I'd like to talk more about our situation." He ran his hands through his hair and started playing with his sunglasses again. "I think that we can make some sort of arrangement."

I arched my eyebrows toward him. "Arrangement?" Unless he could stop this unity, I couldn't think of any other type of arrangement I would want to negotiate.

"With you and Brendan." My mouth dropped open in surprise. "'I know how much he means to you, so I was thinking that maybe there is a way you can still see each other. In private, of course," he added with a forced smirk.

I didn't know what to say. What kind of a guy would offer something like this? How could I possibly deserve someone as good as him? He would allow me to cheat on him with Brendan, and it was his idea? No one is this good, unless…

"Does this apply to you as well?"

He laughed and shook his head. "No. I don't want to date anyone else on the side."

His blue eyes stared through me and I could see how much it pained him to offer this type of compromise. He was right in stating that we had no choice in getting married. His family and my family were the most powerful of all the North American clans, and our union would join us together as one. We would be unstoppable, powerful, and safe. And this man in front of me was willing to sacrifice his own happiness for everyone else.

"I don't know what to say." It was the best I could do.

"Just think about it. We have to be married, but I don't want you to be miserable the rest of your life because you are stuck with me." His voice nearly cracked during those last few words. Without thinking, I reached for him and grabbed his hands.

"You would not make me miserable, Kain. You are an amazing guy with the biggest heart of anyone I know. A girl would be lucky to marry you." He looked perplexed. "You're smart, gorgeous, nice…you're a real catch. Trust me." And as I said those words, I realized that I meant them.

He squeezed my hands and winked. "Gorgeous?"

I laughed and nodded my head. "Yes, simply *gorgeous*. My sister is very jealous of me."

"Is she? Perhaps I *will* consider an alternative arrangement for myself too." He smiled and wiggled his eyebrows, so I punched him in the shoulder.

"Gross. My sister can't count. Besides you can do much better than her." His laugh helped to lighten the mood and within a few minutes, we were pulling up to the departure level of the airport.

Jeffery and Kain grabbed our bags and we checked in without incident. As I was standing in the security line, my heart began to pound in my chest again. This time it had nothing to do with boys, but instead it was the fact I was actually getting on a plane. I'd only flown a couple of times, and every trip cut a few years off of my life. Me and machines that defy gravity do not mix well. Every little bump, twist, and turn gives me a heart attack and a bout of anxiety. I was so busy imagining a crashing, burning plane I didn't notice that someone was speaking to me.

"Miss? Ticket and identification please."

I looked up to see a man waiting to check me in for what seemed like the third time with Kain standing a few steps ahead waiting. He cocked his head to the side and gave me a questioning look. I shook my head and absently handed the security guy my stuff. Once we were on the tram to our terminal, Kain asked me what was wrong.

I felt like such a child, but I told him anyway. "I hate to fly."

He laughed and wrapped his arm around my shoulder. "Well, you haven't flown with me yet."

I didn't understand what he could possibly mean until we were settled into our first class seats with a glass of milk in front of me. The plane was still loading and my anxiety was in overdrive.

"Here," he said and pushed something into my hand. I looked down to see one of those eye masks that people wear to block out the daylight. It smelled like chamomile tea. "Put that on and drink your milk."

"Yes dad," I replied with a groan and he laughed at me. I drank the milk blindfolded, trying not to spill it all over my face, and settled into my seat.

"Good, now just lay back and relax." He grabbed my hand and I squeezed. We started to move away from the gate and soon enough were rushing down the runway and lifting off. It was bumpy and I squeezed Kain so hard, he'd probably be bruised tomorrow.

I heard him chuckle again and I flipped the mask up to give him my evil eye. That only encouraged him some more, but instead of laughing, he leaned in close to my face. "I'll sing until you fall asleep."

I looked at him suspiciously. "Why would I fall asleep?" He smiled wider. "Kain, what did you put in my drink?"

"Omly an anti-anxiety remedy. All natural, don't worry."

Merfolk were the original holistic healers of the world. Our remedies have been working their magic for centuries from the Egyptians to the indigenous people of the New World. Many of the clans had family members who owned holistic centers, health food stores, or alternative therapy practices. And most of those relied upon medicines derived from plants and animals in the sea that humans didn't know had healing properties. I was guessing that my milk had been doused with a mixture of ground up urchin spines and starfish eggs.

"No more drugging me without my knowledge," I said with mock indignation.

"Deal, even though I know you'll thank me later. Now, sit back and enjoy my wonderful voice." He cleared his throat and started to sing *Baby Beluga*. I had to cut him off.

"Really? This is the song you choose?" He ignored me.

"*Baby beluga in the deep blue sea. Swim so wild and swim so free…*" His voice was pleasantly soothing, although not surprising given our nature. All of those old wives tales about sirens leading sailors to their death were not that far off. There was one clan who had refused to live on land for several generations, and they would use their voices and beauty to mesmerize sailors into giving them money and goods. As the shipping industry developed and technology became more standard, they had to abandoned those practices or risk being exposed.

Kain moved on to other songs about the ocean. I vaguely remember him singing about a bump on a log in a hole in the bottom of the sea before I passed out for good. I woke up once with my head on Kain's shoulder and his resting against mine. Even though my neck was cramped, I couldn't pull myself away. I didn't want to. Apparently he could hypnotize me with his voice just as well as our ancestors could.

The flight to Miami was followed with another shorter one to Key West. I was still tired, but couldn't help marvel at the city lights and the views of Cuba from the air. Kain snuggled back against me in an attempt to look out the window too. His warm breath and unique scent continued to relax me, and even though we had moved beyond our usual awkward silences, I was still concerned about spending the weekend together.

After landing and a twenty minute ride in another limousine, we finally made it to our destination. I didn't know the name of the key, but it seemed to be far away from any type of civilization. When we turned off the main highway, a set of large iron gates opened slowly without the driver speaking to anyone. Although it was night, the full moon highlighted the sandy road and the brilliant palm trees lining our path. We passed over a small bridge onto another piece of land. I lowered my window to hear the water splash against the shore and to breathe in the scent of the warm salty air. Kain copied my move and we both grinned at each other in agreement. Florida wasn't so bad. Maybe this weekend could be fun after all.

The limousine pulled over to the side of the road and parked. When I got out of the car, I could see that the driveway continued ahead only to end a few hundred feet in front of a large house. It seemed to glow in the moonlight and I instantly thought about how much it reminded me of my own home. I could see two large wrap around decks and windows encompassing most of the second and third floors.

The driver started rolling our suitcases down a path to the right that I hadn't noticed before. Boulders interspersed with conch shells lined the trail. The large mangroves almost created a tunnel since their braches had nearly grown together. The only sound was the soothing water and the hum of a distant car along the highway. It was incredibly peaceful.

Without saying a word, the driver led us to a small cottage off the side of a dock. There appeared to be a few more just like it further down, but there were no lights on inside. He opened the door and gestured for us to enter. I led the way, followed by Kain and the driver. The boat house was breathtaking and reminiscent of what I'd always imagined an island hut would look like. There was one large open room with a tiny kitchenette, a small bathroom behind that, and one large king bed.

One bed.

We would have to discuss that later, since I was too overwhelmed with my surroundings right now. The ceiling was at least twenty feet high and covered in light wood that matched the flooring. A fan hung from the center with rotating blades that looked like bamboo stalks. On the side wall across from the bed was a brown whicker dresser with a matching mirror and a vase full of fresh bird-of-paradise flowers.

"Pretty sweet, right?" Kain moved up beside me and I belatedly realized that the driver had left. I looked at him and then the bed. It was an unconscious reaction but he followed my gaze.

"Oh yeah. Well, I can sleep on the floor," he stammered.

Waving my hand at him I said, "Let's not worry about that now. I want to go for a swim." I smiled up at him and we had a moment of total understanding. There was also something mischievous brewing in his eyes.

"Race you," he said and took off toward the double set of sliding glass doors on the far wall.

"You're a cheater!" I yelled and ran after him. His clothes were off before he was out of the room and mine weren't far behind. I heard the splash of his dive and tried to think of a way to get even with him.

The balmy air was a wonderful treat, but the warm water was even better. My transition was so smooth it had me wondering if the temperature had something to do with that. Swimming away from the dock, I rushed past Kain who seemed to be waiting for me. I pushed forward with all my energy taking very little time to look around. Our eyesight was decent at night, and the full moon certainly lit up our underwater seascape, but I would have a chance to explore the reefs more tomorrow. For now, I just needed to swim.

I glanced behind me to find Kain. His blond hair reflected the moonlight and I could see that he was just a few tail lengths away. Looking ahead, I tried to find some kind of landmark. A concrete channel buoy caught my attention and I hurdled myself over to it. Nearly five seconds later, Kain's head popped up out of the water and he smiled without showing his teeth.

"You didn't say where the finish line was, so I picked it and now I win," I declared.

A stream of lukewarm water hit me right in the eye as Kain spit in my face. He laughed and I scowled.

"I think I win now," he said. I splashed him but it barely made contact before he was back under the water again. The chase was on.

We must have spent an hour playing around and exploring the shallow shoals until the long flight and late night began to catch up with us. It was well after midnight before we headed back to the boathouse with the great ceilings and that one bed.

This weekend was about to get more interesting.

FOUR

I sat on the back of the dock dangling my tail in the water while Kain took a shower. Phone in hand, I'd sent about ten messages to Brendan telling him that I arrived safely, that the water was amazing, and that I missed him more than anything. He had to work, so I didn't expect a response right away, but I was still disappointed. I needed to hear from him.

I was lost in thought when Kain stepped through the doors with one towel wrapped around his waist while he used another to dry out his hair. He was too busy shuffling his hands around his head to notice me staring. I'd always tried to keep my mind away from him when it involved my hormones. But sitting here, staring up at him in such a private moment, I suddenly had butterflies in my stomach. And they were the kind that I've only ever had for Brendan before.

He stopped moving and caught my eye. "Sorry, I wanted to tell you that the shower was free." We looked at each other a few moments too long before he broke eye contact and pointed to my tail.

"I guess you're not ready to come inside yet," he grinned.

"I've often wondered why I couldn't just live in the ocean permanently. And this," I said gesturing toward the calm waters in front of us, "this makes it very tempting. I could get used to living here."

He sat down beside me and passed me his damp hair towel. Nudity was not something that we were unfamiliar with, and my long hair was covering up most of my upper body but I still appreciated the gesture. I wrapped it around my chest and secretly wondered if it was bothering him more than me.

"You know we don't have to stay in Massachusetts all of the time. We'll be able to go to college somewhere or travel around for a while. Maybe we could come back to Florida."

He was referring to our life post-wedding and I felt nauseous since I planned to run away with Brendan. I couldn't possibly sit here and discuss our future together. That would be wrong on many levels. So I made a non committal noise, shrugged my shoulders, and left it alone. Kain seemed to take the hint and dropped the subject. However, his silence only made me feel worse.

"Do you have any idea what we have to do the next few days?" I asked.

"They really didn't tell you anything did they?" I gave him a look and he held up his hands in surrender. "Okay, okay. I think tomorrow is the meet and greet stuff, followed by some training activities. The ball is Saturday night and I'm not sure about Sunday. They are supposed to give us some free time before dinner tomorrow, and I've already signed us up for a trip to the reef. Granted, we will be going at dusk so we aren't seen, but I still think that it will be cool."

He was always on top of things and it made me wonder what kind of leader I could possibly be in comparison to him. We would never be equals. I wasn't good enough for that. Even though he was only a few months older than me, he definitely had it more together than I did.

"Sounds good," I said and I meant it. This was our first Cotillion, but I'd never asked about his personal friendships before. "Are you going to know any of the other syrenkas here?"

"There's one guy, Vance Donnelly. We met at a gathering a couple of years ago. He's nice. You'll like him."

"He's a Donnelly?" I asked.

"Yes, but not from the Florida group. His uncle is the clan leader, which puts him about third in line."

I nodded in understanding. "And speaking of, how are you doing with all of this. Knowing that you're next up for leadership? Doesn't it freak you out?"

His nervous laugh was all the answer I needed. He was scared and I'd found something that worried him. "When I think about me leading, all I do is torment myself with the reasons why. I will be leader when my father dies and that's not something that I want to imagine."

Now I felt like a total idiot. "Oh, I'm so sorry. I-I didn't mean to imply anything," I stammered.

"It's okay. I said I don't *want* to think about it, but it doesn't mean that I don't have to. His health is deteriorating. We all know it. It just sucks." He laughed again, but it was not happy. "How's that for regal vocabulary?"

I didn't know what to say now. Merfolk typically didn't get sick. Our shifting bodies usually healed broken bones, scrapes, and bruises. The traditional remedies can often take care of the rest. But Harlan Matthew had been diagnosed with an incurable autoimmune disease. I didn't know the details, but it was apparently very rare in our kind and usually shortened the victim's life span by about twenty years. Kain's father had been sick ever since he was born. I couldn't imagine that and it made me very sad every time we talked about him.

"Seems like you're ready for that shower now." Kain's voice interrupted my thoughts. I looked over to see him pointing at my legs. They transformed without me realizing I'd given the command. Shifting the towel around me again, I stood and glanced down at him.

"You're going to be a great leader Kain."

He shrugged his shoulders and tried to smile. It was pretty weak, so I bent forward and kissed the top of his head. "I mean it. There are good things in store for someone like you." He didn't say anything as I made my way inside.

I used my time in the shower to think about my relationship with Kain. We had always been friends, even though I've pushed him away more and more in these last few years hoping that he'd find someone deserving of him. I knew that he was in love with me and it really hurt that I couldn't return his affection. If Brendan hadn't entered my life, I could pretty much guarantee that things would be different and I'd be looking forward to our arranged marriage with delight. But that was not my reality.

When I walked into the large room, Kain was shifting through his suitcase and hanging up a few things. He had changed into a pair of grey baggy sweatpants but kept his chest bare. I was caught up in his beauty for the second time tonight as I watched his back and arm muscles move with grace.

Before he could notice me, I climbed into the bed. I had taken my two piece pajama set into the bathroom so I didn't have to worry about dropping a towel or something and making an already tense situation even worse. He stopped what he was doing when he heard the bed squeak.

"I'm almost done," he said. "I think that I'm going to sleep on that chair out on the dock.

I took a deep breath. "No you're not."

He turned to face me. "What?"

"You can sleep here," I patted the other side of the bed. "I'm not going to sleep in a chair and neither are you. We're at Cotillion for goodness sake. As an engaged couple no less. I think that we can handle sharing a king sized bed. Besides, it's so large we probably won't even realize we're sharing." There, I said it.

He raised his eyebrows and finished folding the pair of jeans in his hands. "Are you sure about this?"

"Yes. It's fine. You stay over there and I'll stay over here, and we'll both get to sleep on the bed." He smiled, showing all of his teeth and exuding a vibe I didn't want to react to. So I tried to cover my unease with a threat. "Do I have to set some ground rules buddy?"

Laughing, he shook his head and put the last of his clothes away. A few moments later, he crawled into the far opposite side of the bed and turned off the light. I was lying on my shoulder facing away from him and I think he did the same.

"Goodnight, Eviana," he whispered.

"Night, Kain."

We didn't say anything after that and although I thought it would be impossible to sleep, in no time at all I felt my eyes close. I dreamt that I was flying through shallow waters like a manta ray. I moved at a good speed over seagrass beds and coral reefs, all the time knowing that something bad was about to happen. Nothing ever did, but that nagging feeling kept looming in the back of my mind and was there even after I woke up. Although I was rested, my stomach was upset and nervous and I didn't know why.

Until I rolled over and looked at Kain's face.

I sat up so quickly that I got caught in the covers. Making a fool out of myself, I tried to detangle my legs and nearly fell out of the bed. I had temporarily forgotten about our sleeping situation, and now my shenanigans woke him up.

"You okay?" His voice was groggy with sleep and I had to close my eyes when he rolled onto his back and stretched out in front of me. *Stop looking. Stop looking. Stop looking.* I chastised myself. The tan, muscled chest kept drawing me in and when I tried to move away, I fell to the floor with a thump.

"Eviana!" Kain cried out. I was on my back with my legs stuck in the covers hanging over the side of the bed looking up into his concerned face and striking blue eyes. What could possibly be any more embarrassing?

"Ow," I moaned and tried to assess if I'd injured anything more than my pride. Nope, just my pride and any coolness I may have had. As soon as I realized this, I started laughing and couldn't stop.

Kain stared down at me for a few more seconds before joining me with his own amused laughter. We stayed like that a little while longer until tears were coming out of my eyes. Finally, he reached for me and I gave him my hands. In one swift motion, he pulled me back up onto the bed. Although I think he underestimated his strength because I ended up completely on top of him in the center of the mattress. I could feel the heat radiating off his chest and my heart pounded.

"Um…thanks," I said, unable to make it much more than a whisper.

"Anytime," he smiled up at me and caught my gaze. I felt his hand push back a piece of my hair from my face and suddenly I couldn't think about anything else. "Why were you trying to get away so quickly?"

The lump in my throat and the butterflies in my stomach made it difficult for me to understand his question. "Bad dream?" I couldn't remember what had freaked me out earlier. What was wrong with me?

His body shook with another laugh while he wrapped his arms around my back. We had never been this close together before and I had never been like this with anyone other than Brendan. Suddenly, Kain kissed my forehead and gave me another tight squeeze. "Well, that's what I'm here for. To protect you from bad dreams."

My muscles tensed with guilt and fear. Guilt because I was thinking about Brendan and fear because I didn't know why my body was responding to Kain like this. He must have sensed it too because he gently pushed me off to the side and rolled out of bed.

"Time to get up anyway. I'm sure it's going to be a long day." Walking gracefully to the closet, I watched him select his clothes; a pair of khaki pants and a light weight button up shirt. The top was sky blue and I knew how handsome he would look in it. I also really needed to get control over my feelings right now.

He bounded into the bathroom with clothes in hand and I heard the shower turn on. Deciding it was too much trouble to bath myself again, I threw on a long blue sundress and pinned back the sides of my hair. After adding a little makeup and some deodorant, I was ready to go. Yet I still sat on the bed for another ten minutes waiting for Kain to emerge. It was clear to me who the female was in this relationship. When he stepped out of the bathroom through a wall of steam, I couldn't help but tease.

"Finally," I sighed dramatically. "I thought that I was going to have to tell everyone that you fell in. Did you get everything plucked and primped just right?"

He looked at me and the side of his mouth curved up with a smirk. "Hey, don't hate me because I'm beautiful. Do you think this hair styles itself?"

All I could do was shake my head. "What time do we have to be there?" I asked.

"What time is it?"

I pulled out my cell phone from my purse and noticed that I had a couple of messages. They were from Brendan and I hadn't even checked my phone this morning. Another surge of guilt raked over me. "Almost nine," I finally answered.

"Then we should go now." He threw his pajama bottoms on top of his suitcase and slipped on a pair of shoes. Holding out his hand he asked, "Shall we?"

I really wanted to talk to Brendan, or at least look at his messages, but I didn't want to make Kain uncomfortable again. So I grinned, took his hand, and prepared myself to play the role of fiancée for the rest of the weekend.

As soon as we walked outside, someone yelled for us. I turned toward the far end of the dock to see a young couple hurrying in our direction. They must have come from another boat house. When I looked around, I could see that there were six different houses along the dock in varying styles and sizes. It was so quiet that I assumed everyone else was already at breakfast.

"Kain, wait up!" The guy was yelling at us and towing the girl, who must have been his girlfriend, behind. She was having a hard time keeping her three inch heels out of the cracks, but not once did she give him a dirty look.

"Hey Vance," Kain said and shook his hand when he arrived. "Good to see you again."

"Yeah, man. It's been what? Like two years by now?" Vance was tall and handsome, as most merfolk were. He had brown shaggy hair that was streaked from the sun and stubble around his lower face indicating he didn't shave this morning. Dark sunglasses covered his eyes and the shorts and tee-shirt were in stark contrast to Kain's more polished look. It was also very different from the girl standing next to him. She had on a one shouldered silver top with a pair of short black shorts. I am an average five foot six inches and she was probably a little shorter than that considering we were at eye level with her heels on. Vance smiled down at me. "I'm betting that you're Eviana."

I looked at Kain with a questioning glance, but before he could respond, Vance picked me up in a bear hug and shook me from side to side. "It's so great to finally meet you." He put me down but didn't let go of my arms. "This boy talked about you constantly when we met. I'm glad to see that you're finally here with him."

He pushed me aside and pulled the girl closer to both of us. "This is Brinsley Kennedy. My fiancée." His face beamed with such pride I had a momentary feeling of sadness. Vance was so excited about their relationship and it wasn't hard to tell by the way she looked at him, that she was in love just as much.

Kain gave her a hug. "Brinsley, it is a pleasure to meet you." Turning to Vance he added, "You finally got her to agree to it, didn't you?"

Vance laughed and punched him in the shoulder. "Told you she wouldn't be able to resist me." He nodded in my direction, "And apparently your charms finally worked as well. Congratulations, man."

Kain blushed a little and smiled at me. I think it was more of an apologetic look. Or maybe it was a "please play along" request.

"Brinsley, I'm Eviana," I held out my hand but she gave me a hug too. They were very touchy-feely, these two.

"It's nice to meet you Eviana. You're from California, right?"

"Yes, around the Santa Barbara area. You?"

"New York. Or really Montauk. Though you've probably never heard of it." She smiled and I realized how beautiful she was. Her long, straight brown hair fell nearly to her waist and her perfect features were only enhanced when she beamed at me or Vance.

"I have. It's nice down there," Kain added and she looked at him with surprise. "I grew up in Boston," he explained. "Sometimes we would vacation there."

There was a sound in the distance that reminded me of a dinner bell. Vance shook his head and sighed.

"We better get going. Can't be late on the first day." Then he added in a mocking voice, "Punctuality is essential in a leader."

Kain and Brinsley laughed while we started walking toward the main house. I ran to catch up with Vance. "Have you been here before?"

"Yeah, Brinsley and I came last year." He waved his arms around with fake excitement. "It's a blast!" Brinsley giggled again and took his hand in hers before looking over to me.

"It's not that bad. Just try to be patient with all of the hoopla. The first day will seem overwhelming, but they'll relax a bit once they see that you're trying to learn." She beamed at me again and I instantly felt more relaxed.

Shaking my head, I dropped back to walk with Kain. "Does she do that to you too?"

He chuckled and wrapped his arm over my shoulder. "Yeah, she's got a special talent for mesmerizing people. It's a characteristic of her family's bloodline. Merfolk with that much skill usually end up in powerful positions. She's a great catch for Vance."

They did seem to be truly happy with each other and I didn't think it was only because of her power over him. Kain thought she was a good catch. I wondered if anyone would ever say that about me. My thoughts were interrupted by another ringing bell and we all picked up the pace to begin our first day of Cotillion.

Five

We were the last ones to arrive at breakfast, and judging by the looks we received, it wasn't the best way to make a first impression. The large open room boasted windows on three sides and a high ceiling with decorative lantern-like chandeliers hanging above us. Four empty seats dictated our arrangement at opposite sides of the table. Kain and I sat down in the closest chairs and tried to make as little noise as possible. In front of us on the dinner plate was a hand printed itinerary of the weekend's events. The gold flecked paper was thick and natural and the calligraphy writing was beautiful. I didn't want to touch it, but once I started reading the schedule I couldn't help but snatch it off of the plate.

"Ridiculous, right?" the boy sitting next to me whispered with a smile. "I thought this was supposed to be fun."

From sunrise to sunset each day, every hour was planned. Today did look like the worst one, just as Brinsley had warned, but I didn't really see that it got much better through the weekend. Listings for interviews, manners, public speaking, and strategy filled the paper and I suddenly felt overwhelmed and incredibly homesick.

"No kidding," I replied. Turning my head to see who was speaking to me, I found a guy around my age who was even more primped than Kain. He had short auburn hair, large brown eyes, and a cute smile. Something about him seemed gentle and I was instantly drawn to his presence. "I don't even know what half of this stuff means."

"Me either, but I heard some of the others talking earlier. Apparently we are here so they can teach us how to be perfect little soldiers." He pointed to one of the lines on my itinerary. "This here, in the *interview* sessions, they make you answer all kinds of questions on the spot with a microphone just like Miss America." Twirling his hand around in the air, he giggled. "I'll be good at that one."

"I won't," I mumbled. Public speaking was definitely not for me.

"And this one that says *manners* means you learn proper etiquette for having business dinners and entertaining other important families." He was practically leaning on me at this point.

"When do we get to go swimming?" I asked.

"Oh, that's right there. Each night at dusk for two hours."

I looked back down at the paper where he was pointing and wrinkled my nose. "But that says physical fitness."

"Yep," he smiled then held out his hand. "I'm Daniel Zane by the way."

I shook his hand. "Eviana Dumahl."

"Nice to meet you, Eviana," he said with a sincerity that was natural and comforting. Daniel and I were going to be friends by the end of the weekend, no doubt. Before I could say anything else, someone cleared their throat.

"Welcome to Cotillion syrenkas. My name is Pegotty Moranis and I will be heading this year's ceremonies." Pegotty was an older lady, perhaps in her sixties, with long graying hair that curled from her shoulders to her waist. She wore a velvet green gown that had black lace trimmings over the bodice and down the front of the skirt. I couldn't imagine how hot she must be in this Florida humidity.

"Our activities will commence in twenty minutes and on your itineraries you will find the locations of each session. We expect you to be courteous and prompt. Punctuality is essential in a leader."

I caught Vance's eyes across the table as he mouthed the words "Told you" and smiled. Shaking my head to hide my reaction, I looked around the room. There were about twenty of us in here, both first and second year syrenkas. The group was evenly mixed with males and females and it was obvious who the novice students were. We all wore a look of fear and distress, anticipating the worst.

Kain nudged me in the shoulder and waved me closer. "Eviana, meet Lily Shannon from North Carolina. She'll be in our group most of the day."

Lily reached across Kain with a wide smile and too much enthusiasm. "Eviana, I'm so glad to finally meet you and Kain. Congratulations on your engagement." She looked up at Kain, which was kind of hard considering that she was pretty much laying in his lap. "You're so lucky." I think that she was talking to me. Realizing what she'd just implied, she hastily jumped back, knocking over a glass of water with her elbow.

"Oh crap. I'm such a klutz!" She grabbed a napkin and tried to wipe up the liquid.

"Here, let me help," Kain said and I could she her blush when he touched her hand. I sighed and sat back in my seat.

Across the table, glaring at me with a look I couldn't quite interpret was one of the most beautiful girls I'd ever seen. She was tall and slim with short black hair cut to her chin, large earrings, and a halter top that showed off her protruding collar bone. I think that she must have been at least part Asian. Her legs were crossed and I could see that she was wearing knee high black leather boots that accentuated the length of them. I didn't want to cower under her scowl, so I raised my eyebrows to silently ask her what her problem was.

Catching my signal, she shrugged and nodded toward the Kain and Lily spectacle. I didn't know what she was implying but when I turned back toward her, she was talking to another boy. Even though I was curious, I made a promise to myself to steer clear of her as much as possible.

In no time at all, Pegotty stood and announced that the Cotillion had begun. My stomach fluttered with nerves in anticipation of what was to come next but when I stood, I tried to exude confidence. We made our way into the small group sessions and the rest of the day was a blur. All of the interviews, etiquette lessons, how to speak, how not to dress, what fork to use first when you're at a council dinner was all a fog. Kain, Lily, Daniel, Carissa (the tall girl giving me looks at the table), and I were in a group together for all of the sessions. Aside from a few hours here and there, we would be sharing in the embarrassment together the entire weekend.

I was surprised that Carissa tended to stay by my side most of the time. She didn't say much to me, but her company was oddly reassuring. I discovered that she was a model in New York, not an uncommon profession for mermaids, and that she had her sights set on Milan. Attending Cotillion was the last thing she wanted to do since her entire summer booking schedule had to be rearranged. We were the same age and she already had a career in place. Granted, I had the fiancé, but neither of those were really part of my life plan. I just wanted to run away with Brendan. Carissa seemed to have it all figured out. She was sure that she would be promised to someone by the end of the weekend and she actually seemed to be okay with that prospect.

Daniel was gay. At least I was pretty sure he was, even if he didn't quite know it himself. We paired up a lot of the time, not only because we got along well, but also since Lily or Carissa did their best to partner with Kain any chance they got. I should have been jealous and maybe I was a little bit. Especially when Carissa was around, but ultimately I hoped that Kain might take some interest in one of them.

"Aren't you excited for the ball?" Lily asked me during one particularly boring etiquette lesson.

"Hmm??" I was trying to at least look like I was paying attention.

"Tomorrow night silly," she nudged me in the shoulder. Her face beamed which made her look several years younger. "At least you're already promised." She sighed and looked blissfully at Kain who was getting too much personal attention from the teacher. "I think that my family is hoping to marry me off this year. There are a few interesting guys here," she shrugged her shoulders, "so maybe it will work out. Regardless, I can't wait to get all dressed up." Her smile was back and I couldn't help but share in her enthusiasm.

"Yeah, it should be cool. I don't think I've been to a fancy event in quite some time." It would be fun to pamper myself, I just had to play dutiful fiancée the whole time. Looking across the room to Kain smiling and nodding at his instructions, I realized that it wouldn't be such a hard task after all. As though he sensed my gaze, he turned his head toward me and winked when he caught my eyes. I felt a slight blush creep up my cheeks and quickly tried to suppress those feelings. I really had to get a hold of myself.

Lily continued to babble on about the ball and her hopes of coming away with an arranged marriage. It still seemed so odd to me. I was constantly fighting the system while Lily and Carissa had not only accepted their fate, but they also seemed to be genuinely excited to become young wives. Lily was the only female in her family and Carissa didn't have any siblings. Maybe that's why they behaved this way.

But as the day dragged on, I continued to ponder the importance of uniting the Dumahls and the Matthews through our marriage. It did make political sense. We would be the largest and most powerful family unit. Kain was cute enough and nice enough, so why couldn't I just accept my fate? My head began to hurt and by the time I had to stand up in front of everyone for my interview session, I pushed all of these depressing thoughts to the side.

The best part of the day came at dusk. Even though our swim time technically counted as physical fitness, Pegotty announced that this was the reef trip Kain had signed us up for already. I was surprised to see that only about half of the syrenka's were going, but when we got to the end of the dock with the awaiting boat, I understood why.

"Where are we supposed to fit?" I asked Mr. Miller who was behind the wheel. The small boat was loaded with coolers and dive equipment. Only Brinsley and Vance were on board and the rest of us were standing there like idiots. Mr. Miller laughed.

"You're not. You guys are swimming and we'll meet you out there." The mischievous grin on all of their faces let me know that they must play this trick every year on the newbies.

"What?" Carissa gasped. "It's like five miles to the reef. I thought that we were done with all training today."

"Training is never over," Mr. Miller replied seriously.

"It'll be fun guys," Lily chimed in with her annoyingly peppy voice.

"It will be exhausting," Daniel added with a sigh.

Vance was still laughing when he waved his hands at us. "Oh, stop being such babies. The water's nice and the swim will be worth it. Trust me." He patted one of the coolers. "Refreshments are on us when you arrive." It was probably just water and fruit.

"What's with the dive gear?" I asked.

Mr. Miller looked around the boat at the scattered tanks and vests as though he was noticing them for the first time. "We have to pretend we need these, otherwise some human might get a little too suspicious."

I looked up toward Kain who was staring off at the distant horizon. Pushing into him a little bit to get his attention, I nodded my head toward the dock by our boat house. He got the signal and started to jog in that direction.

"Where are you two going?" Daniel asked with a squeak.

"Swimming," I yelled back behind me. My shoes were off and I was trying to untie my dress while chasing after Kain. I could hear the footsteps behind us followed by laughing and teasing as the others also attempted to disrobe. In no time at all, we were in the water.

Just like the night before, my transition was relatively quick and smooth. I heard the boat overhead and we all began to swim after it. The five of us stayed in a little group, oblivious to the few stragglers who refused to take part in our childish games. Kain and I took the lead with Carissa close to my side and Lily and Daniel bringing up the rear. The water was shallow at first which made it rather difficult to stay completely submerged. We wanted to avoid the boating channel for obvious reasons, but we still needed to skirt the edges to find deeper water.

After about half a mile the shelf dropped off and the water got bluer. Several sea turtles dodged out of the way, not quite knowing what to make of the five of us. Daniel grabbed onto the shell of one of the larger turtles and tried to let it carry him for a while. The turtle wasn't thrilled with Daniel's game, so it repeatedly slammed his hands with its flippers until he let go.

We were coming to the surface to breathe as a group so that we could all watch out for boats. After one of our breaks, we noticed that we were no longer alone in our activity. Kain grabbed my arm and directed my attention out to our left. The rest of the group swam by us since we'd stopped so suddenly, but they hurried back when they saw what Kain was pointing to. About fifty feet away, swimming around our perimeter, was a pod of bottlenose dolphins.

Kain's face lit up and although I gave him a hard time about this before, he was right when he said that our dolphins were not the same as these. Our dolphins, or porpoise as Kain had corrected me, were much smaller and darker than these beautiful creatures in front of us. I counted at least ten and it was easy to see that three of them were babies.

Carissa swam up beside me since we had all settled down against the sandy bottom to get a better view. I looked at her and saw how enthralled she was. She reached a hand out toward one of the larger females in the group hoping that it would swim closer. I watched the dolphin dart in and out around us, testing to see how much of a threat we were. Nobody moved for the longest time. At home, it always seemed that if I stayed still long enough the animals would decide that I wasn't scary and treat me as part of the scenery.

Apparently, that tactic worked for bottlenose dolphins as well. Once the pod swam closer to us, they would allow a gentle touch or subtle movement. We all started to swim together as one big group out toward the reef. The dolphins flanked us on either side and one adolescent male took a particular liking to me. He kept nipping at my tail in an attempt to get my attention. At one point, I had to push him away to let him know that the biting was getting a bit hard, but he continued to bump into my side at every opportunity. When Kain and I surfaced together, he warned me that the male seemed to have a crush and that I should be careful he doesn't try to take it to the next level. That freaked me out and even though Kain winked, I wasn't sure if he was entirely kidding.

The reef was wonderful and we spent almost three hours in the water that night. Vance and Brinsley joined us and the dolphins seemed to stay around as well. Carissa caught my attention several times simply because she was so graceful underwater. Even though her hair was short, her body appeared to move like an extension of the tresses. Several of the guys in the other group followed her everywhere, but she didn't seem to notice.

Daniel and Lily paired up and explored the rock formations. They told me later that they were looking for lobster. Kain and I swam together the entire time, sometimes holding hands. As it got darker, we made sure that we didn't lose sight of each other because this was when all of the really cool creatures start to emerge. Even though I was looking, I didn't see any sharks.

Mr. Miller blew the boat horn and told us that we were all to follow him in for dinner. They had packed fruit punch and pineapple slices, but my stomach was growling so I didn't feel too bad about leaving.

Dinner was as uneventful as the following day. There were no more embarrassing moments in the bed, and since we had been swimming so much, I had fallen to sleep before Kain even crawled in. Saturday's sessions were basically a repeat of the day before but with the instructors expecting us to remember everything. The interview questions were grueling and the political history lessons bored me to death.

Just before we finished, they gave us a list of everyone who would be attending the ball tonight along with a photo and a brief description of their political platforms. I rolled my eyes when they told us to study up and gave us thirty minutes to cram before an oral examination.

Carissa, Daniel, and I worked together quizzing each other and creating silly names for each person to help us remember them. Lily and Kain were at the far corner of the table and there was more laughing and talking going on than studying. I must have been staring at them because Carissa kicked my leg.

"Why don't you go over there and stop her?"

"What?" I asked, trying to act like she didn't just catch me.

"Please, girl. She's been all over him since yesterday. You shouldn't let her get away with that."

I shook my head and picked up another flash card that we had created. "I'm not worried about Lily." And I really wasn't, but probably not for the reason Carissa was suggesting.

She sat back in her chair and shrugged. "Whatever. It's your marriage."

"We aren't married yet," I grumbled and began quizzing Daniel so that Carissa would drop the subject. It took a lot of self control not to look over toward Kain every time I heard Lily's squeaky giggle.

An hour later, we had completed our exam and were dismissed to prepare for the ball. All five of us were staying in the boat houses, so we walked back together and made plans to meet on the front patio just before dinner. Brendan and I exchange a few quick texts. I missed him and let him know that. He was busy with work, but promised that he had a surprise for me when I got home.

I was so exhausted that I asked Kain if I could take a shower first. Well that and also because I knew that if he got in there before me, there wouldn't be any hot water left. He obliged, and I let the smell of the soaps and lotions carry me away to my happy place so that I could get through this evening.

SIX

I sat in front of the only mirror in the room trying to do something special with my hair. It was so long and thick that pulling it up off my neck and out of my face was a definite in this weather. I looked at my silver gown hanging on the closet door and smiled. It was fun to play dress-up every once and a while.

My hair was almost done when there was a knock at the door. Kain was still in the shower and I was just wearing my pajamas. We weren't necessarily expecting anyone, so I was curious. When I opened the door, an old man was standing there. He had been tall at one point, but now he was leaning over on his cane so much that he'd lost at least six inches. The graying hair and pale skin hung around his face. Dark circles around his eyes created shadows that reminded me of someone who hadn't slept in weeks. When I finally realized who this was, my heart sank with sadness.

"Mr. Matthew?"

"Hello Eviana. May I come in?"

I backed away from the door so he could walk inside. Kain's father had aged a decade since I last saw him. He hobbled slowly and stiffly like every step was agony. I could hear him breathing in short ragged spurts so I went to his side and ushered him to the edge of the bed.

"Thank you, dear," he wheezed. He pulled out a cloth handkerchief from his suit jacket and patted his forehead. "I don't know how people survive in this heat. My body is constantly dripping."

"Can I get you some water, Mr. Matthew?" He looked like he was about to pass out and I didn't know what else I could do.

"Please dear, call me Harlan. You are a part of our family now and I hate the formalities. Yes, a glass of water would be very nice, thank you."

I went into the little kitchenette area and turned on the faucet. From where I was standing, I could see steam seeping out from underneath the bathroom door like a morning fog, but I heard the shower turn off. Hopefully Kain would come out soon. His father did not look well, and I wasn't sure if this was his normal appearance or if he was having a really hard time.

Handing the water to Harlan I asked, "Did you just get here?"

He drank the entire glass before responding. "Yes, I was supposed to arrive earlier today so that I could act as your sponsor, but I was held up in L.A." I gestured to see if he wanted more water, but he shook his head. Upon doing that, he suddenly seemed very interested in our room. He looked around in a circular pattern and when he got back to me, he wrinkled his forehead in concern. "One bed?"

Oh great. Where was Kain? I could feel the heat in my cheeks and the nerves in my stomach. This was not something I wanted to discuss with Kain's father even though our situation has been completely innocent.

"Yeah." I had to clear my throat to get more words out. "But it's not what you think. We have an arrangement. I mean, we're not sleeping together. Well, we are, but it's not like that. We sleep in clothes." Oh, just kill me now.

Harlan laughed and patted the bed beside him. "You are too much, Eviana. Please have a seat so I can talk to you." He looked around again. "Where is my son?"

I sat on the edge of the bed next to him, relieved about the change of subject. "In the bathroom taking forever to get ready." He'd been in there at least thirty minutes now, and even though I was sure that he could hear us talking, he hadn't come out yet.

"Ah, yes. He does take a lot of pride in his appearance," Harlan smiled.

"Sure, but come on. It's a bit girlish."

This time he laughed and wrapped an arm around my shoulders. He gave me a brief hug before pulling away. "I agree. Perhaps you will be able to work on his time management skills once you are married."

My muscles tensed at that last word. I was doing my best to play the perfect fiancée but I hadn't really thought about the actual marriage part so much. That's probably because I had no intentions of going through with this wedding. Looking at Harlan Matthew, I could see that he was genuinely pleased with this arrangement. Our families had always been close and now they would officially be joined. My stomach twisted with guilt when I thought about how much I was going to disappoint everyone.

When I didn't say anything, Harlan gave me an odd look but promptly continued. "Do you know what's going to happen tonight?"

I shrugged my shoulders. "Kain explained what he could. You prepared him much better than my parents did for me."

Tonight was the "coming-out" ball. We would all be officially introduced by family and arranged marriage if applicable. Apparently, a lot of the politically important merfolk would be there to evaluate and socialize with the up and coming clan leaders. From what Kain had said, it's usually a chance for them to begin gathering those who will support their causes and issues. It was just a big schmooze fest mixed with a debutante ball for the single syrenkas. I was looking forward to the food and dancing, but I certainly didn't plan on networking tonight.

"Well, I will introduce you and Kain and then I will join the other sponsors." Each individual or couple had a family sponsor who took responsibility for the actions, behavior, and training of their syrenkas. Since Kain and I were to be married, the Matthew family sponsored both of us together. "It's not so bad the first year. Most of the guests will be meandering with the second year syrenkas, trying to gain political support. You two just enjoy yourselves." He smiled at me and my heart broke. He was genuinely happy for us.

Before I could reply, the bathroom door opened and Kain emerged from the steam. "Dad, what are you doing here?"

"Nice to see you too, son." Harlan tried to stand and Kain and I instantly jumped to his aid.

"You know what I mean," Kain continued. "I didn't think you were going to make it." His father was standing now, so I placed the cane in his hand. "I'm glad you're here."

Harlan gave Kain's shoulder a squeeze and nodded in my direction. "She told me about your primping sessions…and the bed." I must have looked horrified because Kain and his dad just laughed together. Harlan's was a bit strangled, but he was still enjoying himself. "You've got a good one here, Kain. Take care of her."

I was marveling at how much they looked alike when I realized what he'd just said. Kain stared at me with so much emotion that I couldn't hold his gaze. "I will, Dad."

In order to avoid having them see the tears in my eyes, I dropped my head and opened the door. Kain loved me so much and I was going to run away with Brendan when we got home. It would break his heart.

Harlan Matthew shuffled out the door and promised to catch up with us when he could. Kain sat on the bed after he left and stared at the floor.

"Are you okay?" I asked.

He took a deep breath and blew out all of his air. "Yeah. He just looks bad." He ran his hands through his hair, effectively messing up the carefully styled look he was going for. I walked over to him and begin to put the hairs back in place.

"He'll be all right. He's lived with this for a long time and he knows how to handle himself." I finished fixing his hair but before I could pull away, Kain wrapped his arms around my lower back and pulled me into his body. His head rested against my stomach and I thought that I felt him sobbing. Instinctively, I rubbed his back and tried to soothe him even though I didn't know what I could possibly say that would make this situation any more bearable. His dad was dying and from the looks of Harlan, it was going to be sooner rather than later.

After a couple of minutes, Kain abruptly pulled away and wiped his eyes. He stood and walked toward the bathroom. "We have to go soon," he said and then added, "You should put some clothes on." His smile was teasing so I stuck out my tongue and told him to hide in the bathroom while I changed.

The dinner was fabulous. Lobster, fresh fish, shrimp, and conch made up the main dishes with rice, beans, baby potatoes, and a steamed vegetable medley rounding out the sides. Dessert was key lime pie, and although I'd never tried it before, it quickly became one of my favorites. They had served all of us wine with dinner. I didn't usually drink much of anything, but it was good and I had to stop myself at one glass. After all, it wouldn't be a good idea to stumble all over the place when they were announcing us.

The syrenkas were seated at one side of the room, almost like we had our very own kid table. But as soon as dinner was over and Pegotty announced that it was time for our introductions, the room cleared and we became the center of attention. She ushered us to an adjoining room to await our turn. Each first and second year syrenka would be announced and we had a formal greeting to say once we arrived. There was a long open staircase that joined the first two floors and we would have to walk down it into the middle of the room and speak out loud. I was terrified.

"You look really beautiful tonight," Kain whispered into my ear. I had been frantically bobbing my foot and looking around the waiting area making myself crazy with nerves.

"Thank you." I smiled up at him and his blue eyes. "You aren't so bad yourself." He grabbed my hand that was wrapped around his arm and held it there for the rest of the wait.

I could barely hear Pegotty's voice until someone propped open the door. She gave a five minute introduction of which I listened to about three seconds of it. Carissa and Lily were in front of us and Daniel a few spots behind. I swallowed hard when Pegotty announced the first name.

"Liliana Marie Shannon. Unpromised by the Shannon clan." Lily gave a small wave to all of us and then stepped through the door to make her entrance.

"They actually say *promised* or *unpromised*?" I asked Kain.

"Yep," was his only reply. I thought that it sounded rather rude to be introduced as *unpromised*. It made it seem kind of sad.

Pegotty's voice boomed again. "Carissa Ishi Nakamo. Umpromised by the Nakamo clan."

We were up next. I squeezed Kain's hand again and sighed. Why was I so nervous? We were waiting to hear Pegotty again, but a quiet, deep male voice made the announcement instead. It was Harlan Matthew.

"Eviana Anne Dumahl promised to Kain Harlan Matthew by both the Dumahl and Matthew clans." We walked around the door and began our descent. Harlan stood at the bottom of the staircase with one hand on his cane and the other on the banister to hold him up. He still looked ill, but his smile helped to lighten his face. The room was full of adult merfolk dressed in formal attire. The ceiling fans and air conditioning couldn't keep up with the number of bodies and many of the guests were using their pamphlet about the syrenkas to fan themselves.

Once we got to the bottom of the stairs, Kain kissed his father on the cheek and then placed his arm on my back. We walked to the center of the room and he said, "It is an honor to be here. We are bound by duty and family to protect the clans, support the people, and further our existence." He nodded his head and I gave a small curtsy. This was some formal tradition that has been continued throughout the centuries. A syrenka swears duty to the merfolk and basically promises to protect and procreate. It seemed quite a bit outdated to me, but at least they didn't make us take a blood oath anymore.

I vaguely remember hearing Daniel Phillip Zane being introduced, but before we knew it, the formalities were over and the dancing began. It was overtly proper at first, with waltzes and foxtrots. Most of the younger syrenkas stayed off the dance floor at this time, but unfortunately I managed to grab someone's notice.

"May I have this dance Miss Dumahl?" a man about my father's age asked. He had golden blonde hair pulled back into a low ponytail that fell down his back. His light blue eyes were almost grey and completely lacking any shine. I looked up to Kain and he gave me a slight shrug. He wasn't going to stop me…or save me.

"Um…okay, sure." I held out my hand and he ushered me to the dance floor. The music was classical and it seemed to be another waltz. "I don't know how to do this," I said, suddenly aware that people were going to be watching me.

The man laughed and pulled me into the correct position. "Don't worry, I'll lead." His large but soft hand clasped mine and the other went behind my lower back. His hold was forceful but not too strong that I felt uncomfortable. We began to move around the floor, following the few other older couples still dancing.

"My name is Lucian Sutherland and you are Eviana Dumahl, correct?" He already knew my name, so I was a little perplexed with his question.

"Yes, I'm Eviana." We made a few more turns and weaves before I continued. "Am I supposed to know who you are?"

"Oh no, I wouldn't expect that," he chuckled. "I knew your mother a long time ago, so I wanted to have at least one dance with her beautiful daughter." Something about the way he said that made chills develop along the back of my neck. "Your parents didn't come?"

I shook my head, trying to avoid any type of eye contact with him. "No, they didn't. Mr. Matthew is my sponsor anyway."

"Ah, yes. The Matthews." He stopped speaking so suddenly I had to look up. There was something about the Matthews that made my dance partner very uncomfortable.

"You know Harlan and Kain then?" I pushed forward.

"Yes, I know them very well." That was all he would say. It was subtle, but I noticed that his muscles had tensed and he no longer tried to speak with his usual smoothness. At one point I tried to find Kain to give him the signal that I was done dancing with this man, but I was saved by another Matthew instead.

"May I cut in?" Harlan asked. Lucian's hand clamped around mine almost to the point of causing pain. I flashed him a glare and he instantly let go and composed his face again.

"Certainly," he replied kindly. "It was a pleasure, Eviana," he said and then raised my hand to kiss it gently. Something was strange with him, but I couldn't figure it out. Harlan pulled my attention away from Lucian's retreating figure and set me back into a waltzing position.

"Stay away from that man," he said.

"Why?"

"He is very bad news, Eviana. His family is a disgrace to our kind and I'm not sure what his intentions were tonight. He doesn't usually accept the invitation."

We started to dance again, but the moves were slow and small. Harlan used me as more of a support system than ballroom partner. After a few minutes, and just long enough to make sure that Lucian was out of sight, Harlan told me that he needed to sit down. I ushered him over to the section with cocktail tables and chairs. He sat down hard and immediately began wiping his forehead with the handkerchief.

"Here dad, drink this." Kain forced a glass of water into his father's hands started to wipe his face for him. Harlan pushed him away and sighed.

"Go away. I'm fine. Why don't you take your beautiful fiancée for a spin on the dance floor?" When Kain and I didn't move, he sat back in his chair and sighed. "Go. I'm all right." We still didn't listen. "I promise."

He waved us on and I grabbed Kain's hand to pull him away from his father. No sense in giving him a heart attack trying to convince us that he's okay.

The music changed to something more young and hip. It took me several tries to get Kain to focus on the dancing. I even wrapped my arms around his shoulders and nestled against him, encouraging him to move. It wasn't until Daniel, Lily, and Carissa joined us that he seemed to loosen up a little.

"He'll be okay," I said when I caught him looking toward his father again. We were moving slowly together now, so I could feel his muscles anxious with worry. He didn't say anything at first but then he gently kissed the top of my head and rested his cheek against it.

"Thanks."

I hugged him tighter and fought the tears growing in my eyes. This was so hard on him and I admired his strength. I knew that I would not be as strong if I was losing one of my parents. We continued to sway until someone abruptly knocked into us.

"Hey guys, save it for later," Vance said as he bounded into the center of the group and began to awkwardly gyrate his body. We couldn't help but laugh and in no time at all we were enjoying the break dancing battle going on between Vance and Daniel. The moves they were attempting were real, but neither of the boys had the skill to execute them very well. It was quite amusing to see Daniel try for a back spin, only to get around a few inches. Vance attempted a one-handed stand, but when he kicked his feet over his head, he fell on his side with very little room to make it look cool.

By this time, all of the syrenkas had gathered and joined in with the impromptu dance competition. Cat calls, taunting, and superficial threats passed amongst the group all in the spirit of fun. We forgot about our training and responsibilities. I forgot about my upcoming decisions and Kain enjoyed himself freely. For a few moments, everything was good.

If it hadn't been for the laughing and clapping maybe we would have heard something. But the entertainment continued until someone screamed from the far side of the room. The music suddenly stopped and we were all looking around, frantically trying to figure out what was going on.

"Someone call an ambulance!" a voice shouted. Everyone turned their head in the direction of the commotion and the crowd began to move aside and clear a path. At first I thought it was for the emergency help, although they wouldn't have been here so quickly. As soon as I realized what was really happening, Kain ran screaming from my side and down the aisle of people.

"Dad!"

SEVEN

The next few days seemed to drag on through a haze of sadness and disbelief. Harlan Matthew had died before he even fell to the floor. The doctor's declared it was a stroke and assured Kain that it was quick and painless. However, I doubted those words brought any sort of comfort to my friend. His dad was gone and once that realization sunk in, he had a whole other set of obligations to deal with.

We left Florida early the next morning. I was flying back to California and Kain was accompanying his father to Massachusetts for a private family burial. He and I didn't speak much at all after that night. I stayed near his side, helping him fend off the well-wishers and offering my silent support. He didn't cry, didn't get angry. He just moved like a robot. Our friends stayed out of the way, providing only passing glances to show how sad they were for Kain.

He held my hand the entire flight from Key West to Miami, and when we had to part ways in the airport, he kissed my forehead and thanked me for being there with him. Tears rolled down my cheeks as he walked through the corridor toward his own connecting flight, never once showing any sign of emotion on his face. I was worried about him, but knew that his family would meet him in Boston. We would also see each other again in another week or so when they held a memorial service in California for all of the clans.

I felt numb and overwhelmed which made my nearly five hour flight home seem too short. Not once did I think about crashing and burning. Instead, my eyes would well up each time I remembered Kain singing to me just a few days before.

Both of my parents picked me up at the airport and the ride to our house was silent and tense. I didn't want to talk about anything so their multitude of questions went unanswered. Eventually, they realized that they weren't going to get anywhere and gave me a reprieve for the rest of the afternoon. I refused dinner, even when they sent my sister in to coax me downstairs. Tomorrow would be a better day, so locking myself in a room for a few more hours sounded like a good plan.

In the middle of the night, my phone vibrated under my pillow. Sleepily, I tried to make my fingers move to read the message. It was Brendan. I hadn't even called him since I got back and I scolded myself for being so inconsiderate.

You up? He asked. Deciding that I needed to hear his voice, I called instead of texting him back. He answered right away.

"Evs, I miss you," he greeted me and I immediately began to cry. "Hey, what's wrong?"

We talked for a long time. I first explained Harlan's passing and the events of the last twenty-four hours, and soon the sharing eased the pain in my heart so I was able to tell him about the fun stuff that happened as well, like the reef trip and the dancing competition. Hearing his voice was the biggest comfort for me and no one else in the world could provide that serenity.

Toward the end of the conversation he sighed and asked, "Can we meet tomorrow?"

"Of course. I don't know what I will have to do here, but I'm sure that I can escape for a while."

He laughed at that and replied, "I know you can." I smiled. "Why don't you come to my place in the afternoon? I'll pick you up around three."

"Sounds good," I murmured and realized that sleep was quickly devouring me. My heart was at peace for a while and my body relaxed. With the phone still in my hand, I fell into a dreamless slumber.

It was late morning before I pulled myself out of bed and into the shower. Dressed and descending down the stairs, I could hear my parents on the phone, each talking briskly and making a variety of plans. When my mother saw me, she told the person on the other end to hold on and walked over to give me a giant hug. No words, just physical contact, but it was enough for me to know that she was grieving too.

I poured myself some cereal and forced the food down. Clinking my spoon against the edge of the bowl, I stared out the window. Today I was still feeling sad, but it was for Kain and his family. Harlan was a good man who wanted only the best for his son. I thought about his visit to our room before the ball and about how truly pleased he was to have me as his daughter-in-law. My stomach twisted in guilty knots again so I pushed the bowl away from me before the smell of milk made me too nauseous.

"Not hungry?" my father asked pulling out a chair next to me.

"No." My mother sat down on the opposite side across from my father, flanking me with parental concern.

"You should eat. You're going to need to keep your strength up," she chided.

I snapped my head up to look at her. "What are you talking about?" My tone must have been a little sharp because my father placed his hand on top of mine and patted it until I focused on him.

"You are going to be a vital part of the upcoming ceremonies and I would imagine that your fiancé is going to need you now more than ever."

I sighed. "What *is* going to happen now?"

"Well, the Matthews will have the private burial on the east coast tomorrow, but they are coming out here at the end of the week. Friday will be the memorial, Saturday will be Kain's appointment ceremony, and then…" Her voice faltered slightly and she cleared her throat while looking at my dad. "And then on Sunday, you and Kain will be married."

My dad's hand clamped down on mine anticipating my negative reaction. I suddenly couldn't breathe. The wedding had been moved up by a week and I was going to have to marry a clan leader. Kain did need me to be there for him both as a friend and as a partner. Even the childish, angry side of me couldn't argue that point. I let out the breath that I'd sucked in.

"Where?"

"Where what?" my mother asked, looking at me with curious eyes.

"Where will all of this be happing? All of the ceremonies?"

She was still staring at me with trepidation and suspicion. "Here. Everything will happen here."

I nodded my head. Everyone was coming to our clan house and everyone would be expecting me to marry Kain. This wasn't the way my life was supposed to go. "What about my birthday?" Now it would fall the day after the wedding.

"We will celebrate on Monday. My baby girl...eighteen, married, and leading a clan." My dad shook his head and smiled. "You're growing up so fast." He and my mother shared a moment between them that made my stomach ache again.

I stood up and took the cereal bowl to the sink. "I'll be in my room."

"You can have today, but the rest of the week you will be with me preparing for the ceremonies," my mother stated. *Preparing* meant dress fittings, speech memorizations, and a lot of lessons on what not to do or say.

"Sounds fun," I mumbled under my breath as I trudged upstairs. As soon as I was out of sight, both of my parents were back on the phone coordinating the big weekend. This was going to be a spectacle and an affair to remember, that was for sure. No doubt, my mother and her friends were trying to hire the best caterers and the most expensive dress makers around.

I took a nap to help pass the time between my breakfast and when Brendan would pick me up. We certainly had a lot to discuss. Since my parents said that today was my free day, I didn't ask if I could go out with Brendan. When he arrived outside I simply waved goodbye and told them I'd be back for dinner. Closing the door as fast as I could, I didn't give them an opportunity to yell after me. Brendan laughed when I jumped in his car and told him to take off like I'd just robbed a bank.

We picked up milkshakes at a nearby drive through and parked under the deck of his second story apartment. His roommate was at work, and since we usually met someplace where we could swim together, I realized that I hadn't been to his place in a while. It was still messy and stinky, and I made a mental note that I might have to set some cleaning rules when we move in together. That thought made my heart flutter.

I followed him to his bedroom. He plopped down on the bed, which was nicely made up, and patted a spot next to him. We had been together for years, and although we've played around, our relationship had not moved to that next and final level yet. So I knew that his was a gesture of comfort, not necessarily of need. Putting my milkshake on the bedside table, I sat down and snuggled up against Brendan's warm, tall body. We stayed like that for several minutes before he broke the silence.

"So what's going to happen now that Kain is the heir?" he asked. I explained what I knew of the appointment ceremonies and what I thought that my role would be. And then I told him that they moved up the wedding date and waited anxiously for his response. Considering that his girlfriend needed to continue to play fiancée for the rest of the week, Brendan was surprisingly supportive and unaffected.

"Don't worry about the wedding," he said while smoothing my hair as I nestled my head against his stomach. "We are leaving Saturday night." My reaction got a chuckle out of him before he continued. "I can see that you're excited."

I beamed from ear to ear and the relief momentarily trumped the guilt I felt over abandoning Kain on our wedding day. But I didn't have a choice. I was meant to be with Brendan. "Yes, I'm excited!" I leaned over and kissed him. "Is everything arranged?"

"Yes. We're going to Maryland. I've been able to line up a temporary job and I closed my accounts yesterday in preparation. We'll have to stay at a hotel for the first few weeks, but I think as soon as you're eighteen, you will be able to find a job too." He squeezed me in a tight embrace. "We're going to make this work."

"We are, aren't we?" I asked and he laughed again.

"Just pack one bag and collect any of your savings that you can without arousing suspicion. I'm going to work extra shifts the rest of the week, so I don't know if we'll see each other again until Saturday. We will leave in the middle of the night."

I turned my body so that I could look at him. He was so confident and he'd come up with a plan like he promised. I truly loved him and I knew that as long as he was around, my life would be good. We spent the rest of the afternoon together lying on his bed looking at maps and plotting our routes. We would need to stay off the beaten path, so to speak, until I was eighteen and my parents had no claim over me anymore. That would only be for about the first twenty-four hours of our escape, and by then we planned to be in Kansas.

We were heading to the Maryland coast where Brendan had made a contact at a college research laboratory and got himself a paid internship. I was happy to see that he found something he would enjoy. Although he made decent money bartending, he loved biology and at least he could finally put his college degree to good use. It was a popular summer destination, so he didn't think that it would be too hard for me to pick up a waitressing or hostess position. He showed me all of the private coastal parks where we could swim freely and with very little notice. By the time my stomach reminded me that it was close to dinner, I was having a hard time believing that I could get through the next few days. We were really going to do this, and I wanted our life together to begin now.

Before I got out of the car, Brendan reminded me that I needed to act more somber and belligerent. After all, I didn't want to tip the parents to our impending plan. I punched him for the belligerent comment and then tried to wipe the smile off of my face as he drove away. Just a few more days and we could be together forever.

Although I was excited, it really didn't take much for me to realize what this was going to mean for Kain. That thought brought me back into a guilt-ridden, depressed teenager. A perfect cover.

I walked into my house and prepared to play the role for a few more days. Trying to push my feelings about Kain's friendship aside, I vowed to be there for him during his appointment and if I could find a way to warn him about the wedding, I would. It was the least I could do.

EIGHT

The memorial service on Friday was packed and I was pleasantly surprised to see that our friends from Cotillion had made it to the event. Throughout the ceremony, I was able to steal a few fleeting glances at Daniel, Lily, and Carissa who were interspersed amongst their clans throughout the back of the room. Vance and Brinsley had more freedom than the first year syrenkas, so they were able to catch a moment of our time for conversation.

It was much like the other million exchanges I watched Kain go through. Everyone was sorry and they all wanted him to know that they were available to help in any way. Some were much more sincere than others. Considering Kain's new elevated status in our society, it was more difficult to determine who was really on your side and who just wanted to get into his good graces.

I stood next to Kain as he stepped into his father's role that day. His mother was stoic, yet quiet, allowing her son to represent their family with the grace and dignity that she was straining to hold on to through her grief. She was an admirable woman and her total faith in Kain allowed me to see him in another light. Strong, confident, and capable, Kain had become an adult overnight.

The Matthews did not stay at our house. I was secretly thankful for that but tried not to let my emotions show. Just one more day to endure and then Brendan and I would be able to start our new life together. Although Kain and I had acted as a couple most of the day on Friday, we really hadn't had much of a chance to talk. So I was surprised when he knocked lightly on my open door just a few minutes before his appointment ceremony was slated to begin downstairs.

"May I come in?" he asked bashfully. Always such a gentleman.

I was dressed in my gown and just putting the final touches on my hair and makeup. Even though I was to be a bride the next day, my dress tonight was much more elegant than I would have ever dreamed that I could wear. The blue silk fabric clung to my body like ocean waves wrapping me in an embrace. It had a drop waist line that pointed down toward my feet where layers upon layers of fabric fell stylishly to the floor to make it look like I was floating. The top of the dress stretched over my left shoulder and around my neck like a serpent. Gold highlights interlaced amongst the royal blue material and the matching gold tiara with sapphire jewels only emphasized the elegance of the design. I had fashioned my hair up into a twist, allowing a few subtle curls to drape lightly around my face.

I stood as Kain asked his question. "Yes, please come in." Even though I was sure he heard me, he didn't move. Almost a full minute passed before we said anything. "Are you okay?" I finally asked.

Kain shook his head and smiled apologetically. "You look really beautiful, Eviana."

I noticed that he was dressed in the formal leadership attire in the colors of his clan, royal blue and black. The custom designed jacket fit his tall frame really well. The suit reminded me a bit of what a member of a human royal court would have worn centuries ago. Still admiring his presence, he stepped into the room and held out his hand toward me. Not knowing what he wanted, I laid my palm in his a little reluctantly. "I am a lucky guy," he said and lifted my hand to his mouth for a gentle and respectful kiss.

My stomach knotted up instantly and the guilt seared through my veins. I pulled my hand away and pretended to straighten out my dress. "Thanks," I replied with my head down to avoid his questioning look. "You clean up nicely too."

He chuckled at that and walked further into the room, forcing me to take a few steps backward. I quickly glanced toward my closet where I had my bag packed and ready to go. It was as though I worried that he could suddenly see through the closed doors. If he noticed my odd behavior, he didn't comment on it as we sat on the edge of my bed.

"I need to ask something of you," he stated.

"Sure. Anything," I replied, not quite knowing what to expect.

He sighed and rubbed his forehead. "I would like for you to be the one to pin the shield on me tonight."

"What?" I was very surprised. The shield was a small pin fashioned out of gold, black pearl, and pink coral pieces that represented his leadership. Each clan had their own individual design.

It was somewhat equal to high ranking military decorations, but the shield was only reserved for clan leaders. Typically, the wife or husband would have the honor of anointing the new leader by pinning on the shield. In his case, I assumed that Kain would ask his mother. But now, he sat here requesting something very important of me.

"We are to be married tomorrow." I shifted in my seat as he continued. "A few hours does not matter to me. You will be my wife and our clans will be united. There is some unrest amongst us, and I think that our show of unity will let those naysayers know that we cannot be divided."

His suddenly serious demeanor frightened me a little. I had not heard about any issues in the clans and not only did that make feel uneasy, but I also felt inadequate. I feared that I didn't know because I was a still considered a child.

"Won't your mother be upset?"

"I've already talked to her. She understands." He looked at me and smiled. "She's ready for us to be married too." I tried to return his grin but I'm sure that it looked forced. He grabbed my hand and squeezed. "I would be honored if you would do this, Eviana."

Well how could I say no now? "Of course I'll do it Kain."

And before I knew what was happening, his lips pressed against mine in a kiss. It wasn't a quick peck on the cheek, this was a full out passionate kiss. The warmth of his mouth consumed me and I momentarily forgot who I was.

I gently placed my hands on his cheeks as he wrapped his arms around my back to pull me closer. My stomach fluttered and my heart felt like it would climb out of my body. All of the stress Kain had felt over the loss of his father seemed to pour into his movements, desperate for an escape.

The moment seemed to last for minutes, but it also felt like we realized what was happening at the same time. I suddenly tensed and Kain jumped away from me to walk to the other side of the room. The abrupt end to our kiss stunned the both of us.

"I am so sorry. I...I shouldn't have done that," Kain stuttered. His words were muffled through both of his hands which were now covering his mouth like he could wipe the kiss away. "Please forgive me."

I didn't really know what to say because right now I was grappling with the feelings inside of me. I wasn't mad at him. In fact, I had enjoyed that kiss very much. Too much. I walked over to him and grabbed his hands. "You have nothing to apologize for." I smiled up at his apprehensive face. "Like you said, we are to be married tomorrow."

He stepped away from me, however, not before I saw the corner of his mouth curl up a little bit. "So it was like a practice kiss?"

I still felt very uncomfortable, but I didn't want to make the situation any worse. So I laughed. "Yes, that was the practice kiss." He ran his hand through his hair and blew out a deep breath.

"I'll meet you downstairs then," he said. "Thanks."

I heard his footsteps walking through the hallway before I was able to move again. What had just happened? What did we just do? Before I could analyze the situation anymore, my phone beeped with a message. It was Brendan.

Tonight at 2am. Meet me at the end of the drive. Love you Evs.

I almost started to cry. The kiss between Kain and I was wrong in so many ways but most especially because of my relationship with Brendan.

"Eviana it's time," my mother's voice called up from the bottom of the stairs. It was time to play the most important person in Kain's life and time for me to grow up. I brushed all of the anxious thoughts aside, threw my shoulders back and lifted my chin. The tiara had tilted to the side during our little make out session, so I adjusted the crown and walked out of my room.

There was a special area in our house built specifically for gatherings such as appointment ceremonies. And weddings. My mother had added a raised dais at the far end of the room to serve as a stage. There were no chairs up there, only a lone microphone strategically placed in the center. I didn't see Kain yet, but I knew that we were to walk up there together.

Politely pushing my way through the crowd, I made my way to the side of the room and toward the awaiting party. Kain, his mother, my mother, and a few other important political clan members were all lined up and talking amongst themselves. Kain's mother was trying to smooth down his hair and he kept pulling away and swatting at her hand. I smiled at that scene and when he caught my eye, he grinned and shook his head. Nothing like your mother doting over you before the most important day of your life.

"It looks fine," I whispered as I slid in next to his side. He was still fiddling with it as a regal old man took the stage and began speaking. In just a few moments, we were all called up to the platform and the ceremony began. There was a formal agenda to follow that my mother had actually briefed me on. Basically, my role was to stand in the back and smile. There was nothing for me to say and nothing for me to do until the end when I was asked to pin the shield on Kain.

My hands trembled when I picked up the small ornate broach off of the pillow the old man held out to me. I wasn't sure if it was due to the fact that a whole bunch of people had their attention focused on me, or if it was because the shield seemed to pulse with electricity. I never touched a valuable clan item before and although I'd heard stories about them being charmed with merfolk essence and magic, I had always thought that was a fairy tale. But this shield seemed to radiate energy. It trickled through my fingers and up my arms as I looked at it in awe. Kain quietly cleared his throat, bringing me back to the present and encouraging me to continue with the task. I smiled up at him and took a step forward.

The shield didn't have a clasp or a pin and after a brief stir of panic rushed through me, I remembered that it will adhere to the leader without any physical attachments. It was another sign of our magic and birthright, as a shield will only adjoin with its rightful owner. I lifted my hands and held out the broach toward an area on Kain's upper left chest, just above his heart. In an instant, the shield literally jumped from my hands to land on his body. He took in a deep, shuddering breath, closed his eyes, and froze.

The room was silent. Not even the rotating ceiling fans seemed to make a noise. Everyone watched. Waited. I jumped when Kain suddenly let out a sigh and opened his eyes. He grabbed my hand and squeezed, using me for support in front of everyone. His grip was intense, and a few seconds later he released some of that tension but kept a hold of my hand. I moved to his side so that my back was not facing the curious crowd anymore.

"It is done," the old man declared. "I give you Kain Harlan Matthew, leader of the Matthew Clan and Protector of All." Kain stepped forward pulling me along with him. The room erupted in cheer and a few of our friends in the back of the room whistled loudly with delight.

"That was intense," Kain whispered through his teeth. I looked at him questioning his comment, but he never had a chance to explain further. A round of sitting sessions occurred next so that there could be an official portrait of the ceremony and of Kain. It would hang in all of the Matthew Clan houses as well as any official political building. The remainder of the day seemed to passed quickly and once darkness came, we finally had a chance to relax and unwind.

Our friends started a bon fire down at the beach. After exchanging the formal gown for a pair of jeans and a sweater, I took out my hair and walked downstairs to go join them. Kain met me in the kitchen, already free of his official attire except for the gold shield still attached to his chest.

"Why did you do that?" I asked pointing to the broach. I didn't think that he would have to wear it all night. He looked down at it awkwardly while pulling his shirt away from his body.

"I don't know. It was like I couldn't leave the room until it was attached to me again." He shook his head and laughed. "Freaky stuff."

"Yeah, no kidding. Wouldn't it be nice if our elders would enlighten us about more things?"

"Agreed," he said as we walked through the doors, down our large deck, and toward the beach. The night was cool and crisp, and the smell of smoke and burning driftwood filled my senses. It was after nine but from the sounds of laughter and chortling coming from the bon fire crowd, it seemed as though the night was just beginning.

With that thought, my heart froze. This was going to be the last time I would set foot on my beach. The last time I would see my friends. The last time I would see Kain before breaking his heart. Once again, the guilt stomped down to smother my excitement and I didn't realize that I had stopped walking until Kain spoke.

"What's wrong?" he asked.

"Nothing," I said a little too sharply. I really didn't know what excuse to use. He gave me a look and I shook my head. "Really, it's nothing."

He moved his body in front of mine, effectively blocking the pathway to the fire and our friends. "Listen, I know that you are not thrilled about the wedding tomorrow, but I promise you that I will do what I can to make you happy." He grabbed my hands and pulled them to his chest. "I want us to be partners in this, Eviana. I won't keep you in the dark like your mother. I won't force you to stop seeing Brendan." I dropped my head, weighed down by my heavy conscience with the mention of Brendan's name. "We can do this."

"I know," I whispered without making eye contact.

"Eviana, look at me," Kain demanded. I lifted my head and hoped that he wouldn't comment on my glistening eyes. "Please know that I will do anything for you. *Be* anything for you. All you have to do is ask."

I would never understand why Kain continued to place me on a pedestal and hold me in such high regards. It was clear that he was in love with me, and I suppose that a part of me deeply cared for him as well. But I did not deserve his affection or his attention. And he certainly didn't deserve the pain and humiliation he was going to face tomorrow morning. I frantically wished there was some way I could tell him or warn him. But I knew I couldn't and that fact seared through my bones like a hot knife.

"You are a good man, Kain." The words flowed without a filter now. "Please know that. And if something were to happen to me, I want you to find someone else and be happy with them. Don't mourn me. Don't hate me. Just live your life."

"Why would I hate you?" His brows were pinched in concern.

"Just promise me that you will live and move on. Please!" I squeezed his hands harder and pulled them against my body. Traitorous tears rolled down my cheeks adding authenticity to my plea. Kain leaned forward and kissed my forehead.

"Okay. I promise. Now stop crying." He was trying to tease me, but his voice was strained. I took a deep breath and sighed.

"Thank you," I breathed, yet the remorse and fear of his impending pain and heartbreak were still stirring around at the surface of my skin. I looked up at Kain and could see that he was studying my behavior. So much for playing along and keeping my cool. To distract him, I let go of our entwined hands and wrapped my arm around his waist, pulling him toward our friends. "Let's go. They're probably waiting for us."

It took a few tugs until Kain finally began walking with me. He slipped his arm over my shoulder and we approached the orange fire ball. Shadows from the flames cut throughout the collection of mermaids sitting next to each other in a semicircle facing the ocean. We found an empty spot in the sand at the edge of the group, and I sat down while Kain walked to the other side to greet Vance and Daniel. My sister's annoying voice squawked out a laugh and I almost told her to go home.

But then I thought about it some more. She should be here to represent our family, because in just a few hours, I would be leaving. I didn't know what would happen to me in regards to clan politics, but at least they would still have one Dumahl left that everyone could count on.

"What's going on with you?" a smooth, silky voice asked. I hadn't noticed anyone sit down next to me.

"Huh?"

Carissa threw back her head and laughed. "Very eloquent, Eviana." Her longs legs folded underneath her and she held some sort of drink in her hand. "You are going to be the wife of a clan leader tomorrow. Better get all of the one syllable words out tonight."

I think that she was toying with me, but it was still kind of rude. Choosing to ignore my glare, she continued to press. "I saw your exchange back there." She jerked her head behind us toward the place where Kain and I had stopped.

"And?"

"And I wanted to see if everything was okay with you two. Is someone getting cold feet?" Her shoulder pushed against mine and I tried to pull out a smile.

"No. Everything is fine."

Carissa sat and stared at me for at least half a minute before shaking her head. "You're lying."

"No I'm not."

"You are. I know." I looked at her with curiosity. She said that like it was a fact. Like she really could declare when someone was lying and when someone was telling the truth. "There is something going on with you."

I didn't like the way this conversation was going, so I decided for a distraction. Maybe a partial truth would keep her busy. "I'm nervous. I'm going to be a child bride."

She laughed again and the serious look she gave me disappeared. "That's not all that's bugging you, but it's a start. You'll be eighteen in no time." She waved her hand around. "Besides seventeen was practically middle-aged back in the day."

"Yeah, like a hundred years ago," I said with a groan, getting another chuckle out of her.

"What's so funny?" Lily cut in with authentic curiosity.

"Oh, just talking girl stuff," Carissa replied coolly. When Lily looked at her questioningly, she continued in a friendlier tone. "We're discussing her upcoming nuptials."

"Oh! I'm so excited for you!" Lily exclaimed and plunked down in front of us. "Tell me about your dress. Who's doing your hair? Are you going on a honeymoon?"

And so went the rest of my evening. Brendan would be proud of me. I spoke of the wedding with ease, swallowing the ball of guilt each time it tried to escape. For several hours, all of our friends talked, laughed, and shared stories about Cotillion and how Kain would never have to go again. He played along, although I could sense his unease when the topic broached his father's death. No one spoke of it outright, but whenever his new leadership was mentioned, it was an unspoken link to his father's legacy.

By midnight, we doused the fire and returned to my house. Everyone said their goodbyes, but mine were pierced with the reality that I would not see any of them again. Brendan and I would be safest if we cut all ties from our current lives. Besides, once they realized what I had done to Kain and our families, I doubted that any of my friends would ever want to speak to me again.

Surprisingly, saying goodbye to Carissa was hard. She had spent the entire evening by my side, refereeing Lily and Brinsley and changing the subject when she sensed that I was uncomfortable.

"Whatever it is, I hope that you are sure," she said to me as we hugged goodbye. I jerked back in surprise but she walked away before I could ask.

"She's an interesting one," Kain said from behind me. I turned and looked at him.

"What do you mean?"

"Carissa. I can't quite figure her out," he said while staring after her retreating form.

"That makes two of us," I mumbled back. He shrugged and stepped toward me.

"I'm going to go too. We have a big day tomorrow." His mouth curved up in a grin and I had to return it. He was standing there with his heart on his sleeve again. I wrapped my arms around his solid body and rested my head against his chest. The steady beating of his heart soothed me like a lullaby and suddenly I didn't want to let go.

He rubbed his hands against my back in a calming motion. Neither of us said anything for a long time. In fact, I began to get sleepy because his presence was so relaxing for me. When he pulled away, the angry ball of shame began clawing around in my stomach again.

"I will see you in the morning, Eviana. Sleep well." He kissed me quickly on the mouth and then walked out the door.

I didn't say anything. Didn't do anything. I let him walk away knowing that his world would change tomorrow. He would face humiliation and embarrassment, and worst of all, he would hate me. I stood there, with my hand on the threshold, watching him walk out of my life permanently.

"Goodbye, Kain," I whispered and closed the door with a click.

NINE

The darkened skies and quiet streets did little to ease my apprehension as I pulled my suitcase down the road to meet Brendan. The wheels screeched and chirped over every piece of gravel, giving me a panic attack each time I thought that someone might see me. It had been relatively easy to sneak out of my house, especially since it wasn't the first time I'd done it.

My parents and sister were sound asleep thanks to the day's exhausting events. Since my bags were already packed, I only had one more task before leaving. I wrote a note to Kain. It was short and simple, and probably didn't do him any justice, but I didn't want everyone thinking the worst had happened. He needed to know that I was safe and that I wasn't coming back. I left it on the middle of my bed beside my cell phone that could no longer be used to contact me.

The hum of Brendan's car made my heart flutter. He was at the end of the road waiting for me just like he'd promised. The old Honda purred, seeming to approve of our escape. Brendan walked around the front of the car and grabbed my bag, but not before stealing a kiss.

"You made it," he said with an air of relief.

"Of course I did. I wouldn't miss this for the world." My smile stretched from ear to ear as I climbed into the front seat. With one more kiss, we were off, leaving California forever and starting our wonderful new life together.

We drove through the night and nearly the entire next day, stopping only for gas and food when absolutely necessary. Brendan would drive for a couple of hours while I slept and then we would switch. By early Sunday evening, we had finally made it across the mighty Mississippi and into Tennessee.

Driving through the mountains was peaceful and breathtaking. Although we were used to forests and trees at home, this was a different type of scenery all together. I lowered my window to take in the scents of wet ground, cool fog, and crisp mountain air. There seemed to be more conservation areas around than people, so when we pulled into the parking lot of a secluded mountain lodge, I was rather surprised to see as many cars and campers as we did.

"Do we have reservations?" I asked. I didn't think that Brendan had made any concrete plans since we never knew how far we would travel each day.

"Just stay here," he said with a mischievous grin and jumped out of the car.

I watched him walk into the main office and then began to look around. The hotel was built like a large cabin with giant tree trunks making up the walls. It was two stories high and boasted a large deck with a railing made out of smaller tree branches running along the edge. There was a little restaurant on the far end of the first floor and I would have guessed there to be no more than fifty rooms.

Brendan jogged back to the car with a piece of paper in his hand. He opened my door and bowed with a wave of his hand. "Right this way," he said.

I followed him up the outdoor stairway to a room at the end of the second floor. He used the key to open the wooden door and then effortlessly lifted our suitcases inside. The room was exactly what I would picture the interior of a cabin to look like. Light wood planks, that smelled like cedar, lined the walls and ceiling. A king sized four poster bed encompassed most of the opened space, allowing just enough of a footprint for two bedside tables and one dresser along the opposite wall.

Brendan was already digging through his large suitcase that he'd thrown on top of the bed. I, on the other hand, kept staring at the bed realizing that this would be the first night he and I ever spent alone together. Butterflies twisted in my stomach at that thought. We had always been close, but our relationship had not yet gone to the next step. Would tonight be the night? Was I ready for this?

Brendan's laugh startled me. "Come on. Get changed. I have something I want to show you."

"Changed? What kind of change? Where are we going?"

"For a swim," he replied nonchalantly.

I looked back out the open door and into the never-ending landscape of trees, rocks, and mountains. "And just where are we supposed to go swimming?"

He unlocked a compartment hidden at the bottom of his suitcase and pulled out his seal skin. Holding it up in the air he peeked around it and grinned at me. "It's a surprise."

Pointing to his furry suit I asked, "Aren't people going to suspect something when they see a seal swimming in the middle of Tennessee?"

"Not when it's dark. Now come on, let's go."

I rolled my eyes and shrugged my shoulders while closing the door behind me. Apparently Brendan had a plan and I trusted him completely. I found my swim suit and robe, even though both were completely unnecessary for me. But it helped to keep up appearances should someone see us.

It took me only a few minutes into our hike before I wondered again what this plan was. It was dusk at the hotel, but in these massive wooded lands, nighttime has already settled in. I was not dressed, nor did I have the proper shoes for the thirty minute adventure into the forest. There was a beaten path, but it was covered in fresh mud and puddles making it difficult to navigate. Especially in a pair of sandals.

I was just about to ask how much further, when Brendan suddenly stopped and sighed. My foot slipped and I reached out to grab his shoulder before landing in a pile of mud. When I looked up, I could see what he was staring at.

In front of us was a tranquil mountain lake surrounding by a sharp rock cliff on one side and endless forests on the others. The pine tree branches made an archway for us to pass through and the moon highlighted the water's surface like a mirror.

"Wow," I breathed. Brendan grabbed my hand and we walked the remaining few steps to the edge of the bank. Large pieces of rock scattered along the beach area and we carefully balanced on the mini boulders as we made our way to the water. Without saying a word, we stripped out of our clothes.

I dove into the water to encourage my change while Brendan became his seal. The cool water was more akin to our California stomping grounds, but it was much calmer and clearer. Sharp rays of moonlight danced around just under the surface and the depths of the lake reflected back a dark abyss. There were very few animals to see, but it didn't matter. I had never been here before, so the exploration alone was enough to keep me entertained.

Brendan and I swam together, investigating the lake's perimeter. When he is a seal, human communication is obviously impossible, but we were so attuned to each other that words were no longer necessary. Large underwater outcroppings and the animals sleeping beneath soon became our biggest curiosity. We dove and leapt around at the surface not really feeling the need to explore the deeper, darker waters in the center of the lake. It was as if something was telling us to stay away.

I don't know how long we were in the water until he signaled for us to head back to shore. We changed and moved several of the small rocks out of the way so that we could lie on the beach with some type of comfort. Nestled in his arms, Brendan used his seal skin to wrap around our naked bodies. Neither of us wanted to leave yet, so we stayed there, content with exhaustion and the elation of being next to each other. We had found a new sanctuary.

I almost drifted off to sleep when Brendan suddenly tensed. I sat up and pulled the fur tighter around my body. "What is it?"

"I don't know," he replied while scanning the lake back and forth with his eyes.

I followed his lead but didn't see anything. I was just about to say that when I noticed the water rippling slightly in the center of the lake. "Do you see that?" I whispered.

He nodded and pulled me closer to him. The ripples became larger and larger until it almost appeared as though the lake was bubbling from underneath. A dense fog formed around the water's edges and moved like smoky tendrils reaching out toward the area of disturbance. We watched in awe as the fog swirled around in a circle, like a slow tornado, until it began moving in our direction. The forest grew silent and I no longer felt as welcomed as before. But we couldn't move. The sight was too amazing.

From the boiling center of the lake, water droplets began to rise and move together in a pattern like millions of tiny synchronized swimmers. In a few moments, a human shape appeared as the water particles molded with each other to become one. The figure floated in our direction on the water's surface, waving its arms around and controlling the fog. Colors began to materialize in and out of the being until her body appeared almost corporal. Long blonde hair that disappeared into the depths of the lake seemed to have a mind of its own as each piece ebbed and flowed throughout the air and fog.

"He was telling the truth," Brendan whispered and I whipped my head toward him.

"What?"

But he didn't have a chance to answer. The beautiful women in front of us made a noise that was almost like a hiss and a growl rolled into one. She was still on the water's surface and now I could see that her body was at least ten feet tall. Closing her eyes and taking a deep breath she said, "Who are you?"

We didn't move and we didn't speak. I think that we were still admiring this creature but it may also have been due to fear. She breathed in again and then reached forward to touch my chin. Her watery hands dripped down into my lap as she turned my head from side to side. A piece of her hair reached toward me from around her shoulder and grabbed a lock of mine, lifting it out from underneath the seal skin and letting it fall to my back. Suddenly, she pulled away from me with a look of horror on her face.

"A mermaid." Her voice came out in a rush and washed over my mind like a warm blanket. I thought that she was intrigued, but her eyes were wide with fear.

"And you," she turned toward Brendan. "I have not seen one of your kind in quite some time." She stood back up and looked beyond us into the forest. The dancing hair continued to move with a mind of its own while she stayed silent. "Yes, it has been many years."

I couldn't take my eyes off of her even though I wanted to ask Brendan what she was. I had never encountered a creature like this.

"I am a naiad, little mermaid, and I am the protector of this lake." It was as though she heard my thoughts. "I did," she answered abruptly and I swear that I saw her face change into something dark and nightmarish. "Now tell me what you want."

"We…we don't want anything," I stuttered, thinking that it would be better to say it out loud instead of having her pick it from my brain. A ghost of a smile played at the corners of her mouth as she listened to my inner analysis.

"Are you sure?" She was answering me but looking at Brendan. Snakelike arms of fog and hair continued to float around her face and body. I followed her focus and was surprised to see Brendan looking bashful.

"Forgive us for the intrusion, but we are seeking guidance." What was he talking about?

"I would like to know that myself, mermaid," she said while answering my unspoken question.

"My father told me about you a long time ago. We are embarking on a great journey and I would like to know if all will be well."

The naiad swooped down and plucked the seal skin from around us. We dropped to the stones and stared up at her in utter disbelief and in complete nakedness. She rubbed the fur all around her face and body in an almost sensual manner. I turned away for fear that I was interrupting a private moment.

"Yes, I remember him." She hissed while continuing to sniff and caress the seal skin. "I remember him well."

Her head snapped down and she stared at Brendan. It was then that I noticed her eyes. They were almost an iridescent lavender color and I swear that they were glowing. She gently placed the skin back on top of us while wisps of her hair embraced us like a hug. Water dripped onto the pelt making small plopping noises. She looked directly at me again and I saw another hint of fear playing behind those large shiny eyes.

"You have much to learn little mermaid. Your journey will not be long." It was all she said before turning away in a spray of water droplets. Her body disappeared in a mirage of tiny bubbles and endless fog.

"What do you mean?" Brendan called after her. I think I heard her laugh as the last of her figure disappeared beneath the surface. Instantly, the sky cleared and the forest became alive again with a cacophony of chirping crickets and peeping frogs. I was momentarily stunned at what had just occurred, until I remembered Brendan's question.

"You knew about her? About naiads?"

"Kind of. My dad used to tell me a bedtime story, and I thought that was all it was until I found this lake on a map. I figured that it couldn't hurt to check for sure."

"But naiads are supposed to be extinct." At least that was what we had always been taught. Once they inhabited all types of bodies of water, but increased pollution and a growing human population made it difficult for them to survive. In fact all of the water sprite lines had supposedly disappeared.

"Don't tell this one," he teased.

"So what do you think she meant about our journey not being long? Does that mean that something is going to happen or that we are almost finished? Because we'll be at the coast tomorrow."

Brendan ran his hand through his hair. "It's hard to say. They're kind of like the genies when it comes to evading and fortune telling." I must have looked pitiful because Brendan continued to explain. "Neither is known for giving you a direct answer. And usually there will be a million different ways to interpret it."

"So why did we come here?" I asked.

He smiled. "To see if she was real."

"Yeah, okay. That was pretty cool," I agreed. He squeezed me one more time before standing. We dressed and walked the complicated path back to the hotel. The moonlight was barely visible through the pines but our night vision was good enough to get by. I let Brendan lead the way and tried to step wherever he did.

My mind wandered since we didn't speak much on the return trip. Today was Sunday, my wedding day. I wondered how things were going back at home with Kain and my family. Did he get my note? Did he hate me more than anything? My only comfort was knowing that our friends were there and that they could provide him some sort of comfort for a while. That thought made me feel lonely when I realized that I'd also lost all of my friends. I couldn't even tell them about the naiad. It was just Brendan and me now.

It was almost midnight before we made it back to the room. I decided to take a shower and Brendan told me that he was going to go and get us some snacks. We'd skipped dinner to go swimming in the lake, but it had been worthwhile. The warm shower water almost took the chill out of my body, but I suspected that the remnants buried deep within wouldn't go away any time soon.

I wrapped myself in the fluffy robe supplied by the lodge before Brendan got back to the room. He stuck his head around the door and called out to me. "Close your eyes."

"Why?"

He stomped his foot. "Just close them. And face the bathroom." I did as he asked but listened to him shut the door and sneak up behind me. Pretending not to hear him, I stood still. "Okay, open them."

I did. He was standing in front of me in a pair of jeans, no shirt, and with a vending machine cupcake in his hands. There was a single pink candle in the center and a cheap lighter hidden in his palm. "Happy birthday, Evs."

"It's not my birthday yet," I argued. He jerked his chin toward the bedside table behind me and I turned to see that the clock showed that it was five minutes past twelve. Today was my eighteenth birthday. I smiled at him and felt a few tears building in my eyes. He remembered when I had forgotten.

"Make a wish," he said.

I squeezed my eyes shut and wished for happiness. I know that was a pretty vague wish, like asking for world peace, but I just wanted everyone in my life to be happy and content. Especially those I left behind. I blew out the candle and wrapped my arms around his waist.

My head rested against his bare chest and my nerves began to awaken again. We were totally alone and he was only partially dressed. I looked up at him wanting to feel his lips against mine. But when I lifted up on my toes, a piece of cupcake flew toward my mouth. He smashed it against my teeth before I had a chance to take a bite.

"What's wrong with you? Why can't you eat like a normal person?" he teased just before another piece of chocolate was smeared down my cheek. I pushed at him, but only half heartedly because I was laughing too. Every time I tried to snatch the cupcake off of the plate, I would get another smear of chocolate icing somewhere on my body.

"I just took a shower you know," I yelled at him.

"Well, if you would stop smearing chocolate all over your face, you wouldn't need another one."

This continued until both cupcakes from the packet were gone or smudged on our skin. I washed my face while Brendan picked up the crumbs on the hardwood floor. When finished, he climbed into the shower and I collapsed onto the bed. The soft sheets wrapped smoothly around my naked body like a second skin.

I had decided to make my move. Brendan had always been patient with me, but now I was eighteen and I intended to stay with him the rest of my life. There was nothing stopping us from moving forward in every aspect of our relationship now. I heard the shower turn off and my heart climbed into my throat. This was it.

The lights were out but I stayed tucked under the covers anyway. I could hear him playing around in his suitcase for what seemed like an hour before he finally slid into bed next to me. "Are you awake?" he whispered.

In response, I rolled over on top of him and kissed his soft lips. My hands held his head in place and he didn't make any attempt to move at first. "You're naked," he stated between breaths.

"Yes and I'm eighteen." I continued to seduce him the only way I knew how. Soon, his hands began to wander over my body, exploring areas that he was already familiar with and some that were newly discovered for both of us. I had never felt so close to anyone in my life and I just knew that this was right for us. Here, in this amazing lodge, on my birthday. I began to pull at the top of his pajama pants.

His hand grabbed mine and stopped my intentions. "Are you sure about this?" He was gasping for air and I could tell that his control was slipping away with each touch.

"Yes," I breathed into his mouth and any last sign of restraint disappeared from both of us. We spent a wonderful night together followed by a prolonged morning enjoying each other's company and love. It was perfect.

When the time came to check out of the room, we reluctantly got out of bed but still managed to take one last shower together. Breakfast had already ended in the restaurant, so we got on the road and continued on our drive to the Maryland coast. We held hands the entire time. It was like I couldn't get enough of him and breaking contact, for even a moment, seemed wrong. We talked, and laughed, and planned for our future. I was saturated in love and I knew that, no matter what the consequences might be, I was meant to be with this man.

TEN

Three weeks had passed since we first arrived in our new home. Well, it wasn't a home exactly, but the hotel efficiency was good enough for me. We got a discounted rate by staying here for longer than a month, and although it was small and ancient, it worked.

The tiny kitchenette boasted appliances older than our parents. Chipped paint, cracks, and water stains highlighted the cream walls while mismatched tile, carpet, and linoleum made up the flooring. It smelled a little damp and very musty when we first moved in, but with enough air fresheners and moisture traps, the smells were beginning to fade. We hung curtains and a few pictures to make it cozier and it soon became ours.

It was almost time for Brendan to come home. He started his job just after we arrived and every day was an adventure for him. The smile on his face was enough for me to see how much he truly enjoyed this new life. I, on the other hand, had not been able to find a job yet.

There were a few promising call backs, but most of the summer staff had been hired months earlier. The best I could hope for was something part-time or temporary.

Although I enjoyed playing house with Brendan and cooking dinner when he came home, I was going stir crazy. We hadn't been able to go swimming very much and that was impacting both of us. The changes were a necessary part of our existence...much like eating. It nourished and replenished our bodies and kept us strong and healthy both physically and mentally. I would get anxious and Brendan would get sick if we postponed our changes for too long. The bathtub could always work as a temporary solution, but our little residence did not have the room for one.

"Evs, I'm home!" Brendan called from the door.

I rushed over to him and jumped into his arms. My kiss muffled his laugh as I tried to focus on the smell of his sweat and ignore the dead fish aroma that saturated his clothes every evening. He held me in his arms long enough to reach the bed, which was only a few steps away from the front door. Collapsing down as one, we giggled as our heads slammed together and completely ruined the romantic moment.

"Are we ever going to get the hang of this?" I asked while rubbing the spot where I was sure there would be a bump in a few hours. In response, Brendan rolled on top of me and kissed my injury.

"Yes, we will." I drew his face down to mine for a longer kiss before he pulled away. "Plus, we have the rest of our lives to figure it out," he said although the words were muffled against the warmth of my lips.

His green eyes stared directly through my heart and I could see in them how much he loved me. Every time I worried about Kain and my friends from home, one look like this from Brendan would brush my anxiety away.

Pushing himself up from the bed, he removed his shoes and his shirt. His hands moved down his sides to slowly unbuckle his belt and I watched with fascination and hunger as he lowered his shorts to the ground. I thought that his little strip tease was for me until he walked into the bathroom and turned on the shower.

I threw my arms out to the side of the bed and let out a loud sigh of frustration. His laughter echoed through the tiny room like a chastity belt locking down my raging hormones. I would make him pay for this later.

While plotting my evil ways, I made us a quick spaghetti dinner as I was hoping that we could swim tonight. It didn't take much to convince him, and once the sun succumbed to the awaiting night, we headed to the beach.

Since seals weren't so common in this part of the country and mermaids were just a fairy tale to humans, we needed to be careful that we weren't seen. Night swims were pretty much the only way to guarantee privacy and safety, even though I was dying to explore the warmer east coast waters during the day.

We stopped the car at the park entrance and walked through the dunes to an area typically blocked off to swimmers. The rough rip current and large rock jetties made this a dangerous place for humans and an unattractive spot for fishermen. But it was perfect for us.

Stripping quickly, we ran to the water's edge and I watched as Brendan slipped into his seal skin. It was so graceful and natural for him and the ease in which he transformed always fascinated me. In less than a few seconds, his furry vertical body sat next to my feet. I looked down into his green eyes and smiled.

"You know that you look like my pet right now?" I said while rubbing the top of his head. He snorted and pushed against the side of my leg. I wiggled a finger at him. "Now, now. Behave Fido or I'm taking you home." That earned me a nip on the ankle and before I could retaliate, he disappeared into the water.

The breaking waves pierced the quiet night with the slaps and murmurs of water from distant places. A cool breeze rustled past my face soothing me yet also causing my senses to suddenly tense. There, underneath the smell of the sea, was something familiar yet unidentifiable. It was almost the scent of another being, but I couldn't quite place it. Goosebumps rose up along the back of my neck and chills trickled through my body. I looked all around us down the beach and behind on the sand dunes. There was no one there.

Brendan's seal voice broke my concentration, his grunting and chirping a sign that he was waiting for me. Ignoring my concerns and trying to convince myself that we were alone, I dove into the first wave I could reach and let my body adapt to its second home.

From the moment I felt the waves envelop me in their embrace, I knew that something was wrong. The underwater world vibrated with an unfamiliar energy. It was dark, my senses were heightened, and we were not the only two out swimming tonight.

A shadow darted over my head but quickly disappeared into the darkness. I stopped moving forward and frantically turned in circles to see if I could identify our guest or try to find Brendan. There was nothing but a sandy bottom below and black water all around. With the moon only a sliver, it wasn't big enough to provide light for me to identify the animal that just made a horrible shriek nearby.

I swam to the surface to catch my breath and survey the damage. Surely something had just died, but the calm seas didn't give away its secret. Diving back down to the bottom I remained still, listening and sensing for something, some sign that Brendan was all right.

It seemed like minutes passed before I heard his signature snorts coming toward me and closing in fast. Brendan dashed from the dark waters and crashed into my body. His flippers pinned me down to the ground, but his eyes scanned the emptiness around us.

A faint ray of moonlight pierced through the depths and I thought I saw a piece of his fur floating in the water, hanging on by only a thread of skin. Looking more closely, I noticed that he did in fact have a large section of his shoulder ripped apart, exposing pink, muscled flesh underneath. What could have possibly caused this injury?

I reached up to put the skin back where it belonged, but Brendan grunted and snapped his teeth at me commanding me to stop. His weight crushed me and at the first moment I could, I kicked out from underneath him and spun my body around to face the oncoming danger.

But when I turned, there was nothing. No shadows, no bodies, and no enemy. Brendan continued to lie in a guarded position on the sea floor, so I ventured a few kicks away ignoring his warning noises. I didn't breathe underwater, so my sense of smell was useless. I tried to feel for those electrical pulses and listen for movement in the water column.

However, they were too quick. Three dark shapes rushed out of the blackness from the side. I couldn't tell what they were exactly, but they were large and they were fast. They swam directly toward Brendan and attacked him with such savagery and quickness that I couldn't react at first. He was screamed, which is one of the most horrifying sounds in the world coming out of a seal's vocal chords.

I watched him snarl and bite his attackers in pure rage. He was larger than they were, but he was outnumbered. The brutality of the fight seemed surreal until one of them sank their jaws into Brendan's already injured shoulder and yanked a piece of flesh off of his body.

That knocked me out of my paralysis and I tried to swim to his aide. I only got a few feet when something sharp and painful sliced into my tail. Screaming in frustration I whipped around to see what had happened, and found myself staring into the green eyes of another large seal.

Stunned, I froze for a moment absorbing what my brain refused to accept. This was not a regular seal. This was another selkie and I belatedly realized that's what I smelled earlier on the beach.

His fangs plunged into my tail again ripping my thoughts back to the present. Shouting, I lunged forward and punched him in the face. The force of my counter-attack must have surprised him because he let go of me and swam back a few feet. We circled each other like lions ready to fight for their territory, each one waiting for the other to make the first move. In the background, I could see Brendan and the other selkies rushing around us in a game of cat and mouse. But me and my seal only had eyes for each other. His biggest weapon was his teeth, but I had arms and hands and I was willing to fight as long as I needed.

When I heard Brendan's tortured cry again, I made my move. Dodging in with a quickness unmatched by any seal, I reached forward and wrapped my arm around his neck. Trying to avoid his attacking fangs, I was able to swing around behind him, effectively putting the selkie in a choke hold. Seals were typically smaller than me, but this one had a large neck, full of muscles and skin, making it difficult for me to get a good grip.

He thrashed and turned, trying to knock me away. But I didn't let go. Another painful scream echoed through the currents, and even though I didn't know if it was Brendan's, it gave me the burst of energy I needed.

I squeezed tighter and fought through my throbbing muscles and injured tail. The selkie at my mercy began to fade. I wouldn't be able to kill him like this, but I'd at least hoped to knock him out long enough to grab Brendan and get out of the water. Yet before I could finish the job, the three selkies that had attacked the love of my life swam cautiously toward us.

My eyes flitted around frantically searching for Brendan. When I spotted him lying on the sandy bottom several feet away, my arm tightened around the seal as his friends slowly encircled me. I might have been able to subdue one selkie thanks to my experience with Brendan, but I knew that I was no match for three more. Perhaps they would take my surrender.

Pushing the nearly unconscious seal from my grasp and toward one of his buddies, I put my arms up in submission and slowly started to back away. They looked at me with concern and fear in their eyes, but they didn't seem to be inclined to attack. I realized too late that Brendan had really been their only target. Two of them grabbed their friend's flippers in their mouths and swam him to the surface.

The last selkie watched me with intent and something else. Maybe fascination or even curiosity. I couldn't tell. All I cared about was getting to Brendan.

I moved back enough so that I was directly over top of my boyfriend's lifeless body. Looking down at him took all of my remaining strength. He couldn't die now. I needed him too much.

When I lifted my head again, the remaining seal had disappeared. Spinning around in several circles, I searched for our attackers with all of my senses, but they were gone. I quickly sank to the sea floor next to Brendan. He wasn't dead, but he wasn't in good shape either. He needed to shift as soon as possible to help heal his injuries. It was hard to see exactly what had happened to him in the darkened waters although I noticed blood seeping from his skin. He had to get to shore.

Wrapping my arms underneath his flippers and holding him in a backward hug, I picked him up and started kicking toward the surface. He was heavy and unable to help much, but eventually we made it to the top. I sucked a large breath of air into my stinging lungs, relishing in the shards of pain that let me know I needed it. In contrast, Brendan's breaths were shallow and quick but at least he was still breathing.

Using every last bit of strength I had, I began to pull us to the shoreline. Once we reached the breaking waves, I focused on my change. It was hard and painful since my energy was gone and my emotions were frantic. My change took way to long and I tasted blood in my mouth from biting my lip several times as my legs reformed around the scarring puncture wounds. It would take at least a day for those injuries to heal.

Looking over at Brendan, I took a more concise inventory of his wounds. The shoulder tear from the first assault wrapped around to the front of his chest. The fur was barely attached in several places, exposing pink, bloodied skin underneath. He had multiple bite and tear wounds all over his body and a large gash down his face from the bottom of his left eye to his throat. They were literally trying to kill him.

I cried while I dragged him through the remaining ocean and onto the beach. It took a while, but eventually I pulled him in between two sand dunes where we were protected both from anyone on the beach and the selkies that had attacked us in the ocean.

"Brendan," I whispered while shaking him slightly. "Brendan, you need to change." I knew that was asking a lot of him considering the condition he was in, and his muffled return grunt let me know that he felt the same way. "I know it's going to be hard, but you have to heal." His response was just a sigh this time. Frustrated tears flooded my eyes again. I couldn't rip the skin from him and force his change, it didn't work that way. "Brendan!"

I could almost feel the ripple of magic trickle around him. He suddenly let out a wail so heartbreaking that I cursed the world for not allowing me to do more for him. His body began to shake violently and the screaming turned into whimpering. Every time he twitched, I could hear another snap or crack as his body shifted from seal to human.

This wasn't normal for him, and I was consumed with the worry that something might not transition incorrectly. It went on for at least ten minutes; screaming, breathing, crunching. I knew how painful my transitions always were, but this was like nothing I could imagine.

Finally, the pelt collapsed around his human body and he shuddered with the last of his strength. "Eviana..." he barely whispered.

I pulled the skin away from him and gasp in horror as I took in the scene in front of me. Every wound, every bite, every tear was amplified in his human form. Usually, shifting helped him heal the worst of an injury. But Brendan's body was so weak that his energy was put toward the change and there was nothing left to spare for the healing.

I couldn't move him right now without risking more pain, so I decided that we would stay here and rest until he could regain some of his strength.

I left him lying on the beach for just a few moments so I could leave our protected dune and look for any potential enemies. The calm sea was only interrupted by the breaking waves as there was no one around for miles. Although I knew better than to think we were safe, I thought we could at least rest for a while without any intrusions.

Making my way back to Brendan, I realized how exhausted and hurt I was. Both of my legs had been bitten badly and blood leaked from the tiny puncture wounds. I couldn't do anything about that right now other than leave them alone. In a few hours, I was sure the pain would worsen as they healed from the inside out, but I would survive. It was Brendan I needed to worry about.

Reaching down, I lifted the tattered piece of seal skin that was the secret to his existence. Tears threatened my eyes again as I looked at the rips and tears. He was lucky to be alive, and the fact that he had been able to transition let me know he was stronger and more powerful than I'd ever imagined. I placed the skin on the dune to my left to allow both the blood and the water to dry.

Brendan was on his side, still in the same position I'd put him in, so I slowly slid down beside him. Exhaustion quickly overwhelmed my body and as I snuggled up against his back my eyes began to close. *Just a quick nap and then I will get us home*, I thought. My arm instinctively wrapped across my selkie's body, protecting him from whatever else was out there. They were not going to get him again.

It was the last thought I remembered before blackness swarmed into my mind and closed it off to the world.

I awoke with a start like something had pulled me from my unconscious state with a purpose. It was still dark but the hint of dawn shimmered on the distant horizon. The stars had disappeared near the water's edge, replaced instead by a dim sheen of purplish blue haze. We probably had an hour before sunrise.

I cursed myself for allowing us to sleep so long. Remembering why we were still here, I rolled over to study Brendan. His breathing was strong although his wounds were still prevalent. It looked like the bleeding had stopped, but the slightest movement might open up the worst of his injuries again.

"Evs?" he questioned through his sleepy stupor. I ran my hand through his hair and leaned down to give him a kiss on the cheek.

"I'm here, Brendan."

"Are we still on the beach?" He started to sit up, but stopped suddenly when the pain seemed to get the best of him. Taking a deep breath, he closed his eyes and fought to continue. I wanted to help him, but I knew that he would want to do this alone. He needed to prove something to himself right now. I would be there to help him later. Blinking his eyes several times, Brendan's attention focused on the far eastern horizon. "It's almost dawn."

"Yes, and we need to get home. Do you think that you can make it to the car?" He nodded curtly and began to push himself to standing. I grabbed his left arm to help steady him and for the first time in the disappearing darkness, I saw the extent of the damage to his back and right shoulder. Sand grains were embedded into the wounds and I knew that it would take us hours to clean them out. But for now, we had to get home and off of this beach.

"Let me grab our clothes," I said knowing that we couldn't walk back to the car and drive to our hotel completely naked. Jumping over the closest dune, I ran to the spot where we had dumped our clothes the night before. I pulled the sundress over my head and decided that we were lucky Brendan had grabbed a loose tee shirt and shorts on his way out the door yesterday. Hopefully they wouldn't irritate his injuries to much.

When I got back to our dune hiding place, Brendan was standing but walking around in circles searching for something. "Where is it?" he asked without looking at me.

"What are you talking about?"

"My skin!" he yelled. "I can't find it!" My stomach dropped in dread before I could get a hold of my emotions. I stepped closer to him, fearful that he was going to lash out again.

"I put it over here on this dune," I replied calmly, pointing to the area behind us. He stumbled over to the dune, falling twice before reaching it. I never saw him like this before and it scared me just as much as it worried me.

"It's not here! It's not here!" he screamed and the panic in his voice shook me to the core. I ran over to the spot where I had gently laid out the skin just a few hours ago and saw nothing.

"No, no, no," I mumbled. Scrambling up the dune's face, I fought against the falling sand to climb to the top. I couldn't believe what I was seeing, but what I smelled was unmistakable. Interspersed with Brendan's fur and blood scent was the aroma of another selkie, one of the seals that had attacked us. The human footprints were unmistakable and the trail that headed away from the skin could mean only one thing. "No," I whispered this time. Why did I let us stay here? I whipped my head back down the dune toward Brendan who was sitting on the edge panting and looking up at me with frantic eyes.

"They took it, didn't they?" I slid down the sand and stopped in front of my boyfriend.

"I'm so sorry, Brendan! You couldn't move and I was exhausted. I thought I hid us well enough, but I fell asleep. I fell asleep and now it's gone." I was sobbing and as much as I wanted to wrap my arms around Brendan, I knew that it would only cause him more pain. He looked down at me with absolutely no expression on his face. It was probably the worst thing that he could have done and I suddenly knew things had changed between us.

"We need to go," he said sharply.

Yes, maybe we could track them down. I pushed to my feet and reached out to him. Surprisingly, Brendan grabbed my hand and squeezed. "I have to get home."

"We're not going after them?" I asked. He let out a muffled laugh, sending chills through my body.

"We'll never find them."

He didn't say anything else as he slipped on his clothes and started walking back toward the car. I knew that a selkie could live for a while without their skin, but with consequences. There were a thousand questions racing through my head and we would have to talk about them soon. However, I understood well enough that now was not the time. We would give him a chance to heal and then we could go after the selkies that attacked us.

ELEVEN

A full day passed before Brendan was able to stay awake for more than an hour at a time. At least when he was sleeping, I was able to tend to his wounds. Some of the smaller scrapes and bruises healed, but he was unable to move much of his right side and his face was still swollen around the gash that bisected his cheek.

I called his new boss and told him that Brendan had the stomach flu and would most likely be out for a few days, hoping that would buy us some time. But what I really wanted to do was go after those that had attacked us and retrieve the skin.

I was making a small dinner when I heard Brendan stir on the bed. Bringing him a glass of water, I sat down on the edge and looked at his pale face.

"How are you feeling?" I asked.

"I've been better," he said with a strangled smile.

"Are you well enough to talk?" We hadn't been able to develop a plan or discuss the attack yet and I was anxious. He squeezed my leg and sighed.

"Let's eat first."

So we did. I made up his favorite plate of grilled chicken, spinach, and tomatoes and helped him with each bite. The food seemed to instantly give him strength and a small part of that tight knot in my stomach began to unwind. Maybe he would get through this without his skin after all.

"So how much of the mermaid-selkie relationship do you know?" he started suddenly, surprising me with the topic.

"Um, well I remember some of the stories they told us when we were young about those who could call the selkies and other water creatures under their spells. But it's more like the human fairy tales about mermaids drowning love-sick sailors. It's just a story and it's obvious that it isn't possible," I replied while waving my hand back and forth between us to indicate our special relationship. "I don't control you."

His swallowed a forced laugh and shook his head. "No you don't. But you are not a leader." I glared at him for that remark. "You are not a leader *yet*," he edited.

"What do you mean?"

"Selkies don't live together or hunt together. We are an independent bunch, only seeking human companionship for the purposes of fostering a child. The selkies that attacked us were commanded to do so."

I nearly choked on my food. "By *mermaids*? That's not possible."

"There was a reason they didn't hurt you more, Evs. Either they were told to leave you alone or they are incapable of hurting a mermaid."

"But they did attack me," I reminded him.

"Not like they attacked me," he replied solemnly. He was right, but I still couldn't wrap my brain around what he was implying.

I set our plates down on the floor while trying to formulate my next question. "So you're telling me that there's a pack of selkies out hunting…what? Other selkies? And that they are doing this under the command of a mermaid clan leader? That seems a bit ridiculous, don't you think?" I could barely contain the sarcasm tainting my comment.

"I think that there are a lot of things that your mother kept from you," he said with a hint of pity. "I've been on my own since I was sixteen, but before I left my father, he had one warning for me."

"And that was…" I said, asking the question he wanted me to voice.

"Stay away from mermaids."

I stared at him in disbelief for what must have been a full minute before bursting into laughter. "Well, you really blew that one didn't you?" I squeezed out between giggles. "I guess we're not all that scary now are we?"

Brendan reached out for me again and I snuggled into his arms with my back against his chest. "You aren't." He kissed the top of my head and sighed. "But we need to find out who's controlling the selkies on the east coast. And if we figure that out, then maybe we can get my skin back."

"And just how are we supposed to figure that out?" I asked skeptically.

"You will need to talk to your mother."

I jumped away from his arms so fast the room spun around me. "What? No way!"

"Fine. Kain might be able to help too. But you need to talk to one of them." I stared at him with my mouth hanging open in disbelief while he continued to speak of crazy things. "We have to find out who is powerful enough to control the selkies. I don't know anyone around here and considering the warm welcome I received last night, I doubt that another selkie would be able to get close to us without trying to kill me."

I shook my head and began pacing the room. "You know that's impossible, Brendan. I *left* him. On our wedding day. I doubt that Kain or any of my friends will ever talk to me again." I ran a hand through my hair and tucked a stray strand behind my ear. "Besides, my mother probably shunned me."

"Don't be silly. She wouldn't shun you. Didn't you say that practice hasn't been used in several centuries?" he asked jokingly.

"Yes, but it's my mother and I'm sure that she will never forgive me for the embarrassment I brought to my family."

"Evs…" Brendan tried to reassure me.

"There has to be another way, okay? Just let me think about it. Maybe there's someone else I could contact." I thought about Daniel or even Carissa. But if my mother really did shun me, I could get them in a world of trouble just for speaking with me. Besides, I wouldn't even know how to get in touch with them anymore. My cell phone was gone and the only numbers back home that I knew by heart were my parents and Kain's. "I'll figure something out."

Brendan suddenly began to cough and I rushed to his side in a panic. He tried to wave me away, but when his hand pushed against my arm, I felt something sticky cover my skin.

"You're bleeding!" I yelled at him. There were several smears of blood around his face where he had tried to stop the coughing. "Why are you spitting up blood?" I asked in desperation. He shook his head and took several deep, soothing breaths as the coughing fit subsided and he regained his composure.

"It's the skin," he panted. "The sickness."

I stared at him in confusion for a moment. "But I thought that took weeks before you would start feeling bad?"

"Yes," he pushed out. "But I'm already weak…" His eyes began to drift shut again and I reached over to pull his head close to my face.

"Brendan. Brendan!" I shook him a little bit, not caring about the pain I may be causing. I was scared and I didn't know what was happening to him. "Brendan, wake up!"

A shadow of a smile pulled at the corner of his lips and I let out a sigh of relief. "I'm okay, Evs. I just need to rest." Kissing the top of his head, I let him lay back and fall asleep again.

I walked to the kitchen to grab a wet towel, all the while thinking about what was happening. My incompetence over protecting Brendan and his seal skin may now cost him his life. I had already ruined any semblance of a family when I chose to run away, and now the only person in my life was getting closer to death at an alarming speed.

Why would a mermaid command selkies to kill? What would be the benefit?

While gently wiping the blood off of Brendan's sleeping face, I tried to step into the mindset of a clan leader. Kain had mentioned that there was political unrest amongst some of the clans, but this couldn't possibly be related, right? Stealing the skin of a selkie doomed them to a life on land and would eventually kill them. How could the death of one lone selkie be a factor in mermaid politics? It just didn't make sense. Brendan was right in suggesting that Kain may be able to shed some light on the situation, but contacting him for the sole purpose of asking for his help was out of the question. How could I possibly do that to him? I already felt bad enough.

Two more days passed, albeit slowly and painfully. Brendan's conditioned worsened and he spent most of the time sleeping or coughing. The wounds didn't get any worse but it seemed as if his healing had stopped. My selkie's normally tan, taut skin withered and paled like a rotting apple. The spark in his beautiful green eyes hid behind the tragedy of the situation, only peeking through briefly when he smiled at me.

I was still unable to come up with a solution and today I decided to put my feelings and fears aside and do what I could to save Brendan. Using a prepaid cell phone that we purchased just after our arrival, I locked myself in the tiny bathroom and slid down to the uninviting floor.

My heart hammered in my chest, threatening to escape its boney enclosure. I needed to get a handle on my emotions before I could make the call. It took thirty minutes. Thirty minutes of me sitting on the cold tile floor with my back pressed up against the dollhouse sized vanity, sweating and shivering with dreaded anticipation. Thirty minutes trying to decide if I was making the right choice. Finally, I dialed the familiar number and sucked in a breath.

"Hello?" the voice asked in trepidation. When I didn't say anything it continued pressing, "Who is this?"

"K-Kain," I stammered. "It's Eviana." The deathly silence on the other end of the line cut through my heart like a thousand tiny glass shards. He hated me. I never should have called.

"Evaina," he said after a full minute of silence. "Where are you?" He was curious, I could tell, but he wasn't asking out of concern for me and my safety. That was clear by his tone.

"In Maryland," I replied softly.

He made some sort of noise that sounded like a laugh but it was way too wicked. "Couldn't get far enough away, could you?"

I swallowed the giant lump in my throat and tried unsuccessfully to stop the tears. "Kain, please don't do that."

"Do what?" he snapped. "It's bad enough that you ran away, but to find out that you ran all the way to the opposite side of the country? What am I supposed to say?" He was so angry and hurt and I deserved every bit of his wrath. I wasn't denying that fact, but knowing it didn't take the sting out of hearing him vent his frustrations with me. "Do you even have any idea how much trouble you've caused for our families? Your mother shunned you, Eviana. *Shunned* you! I would be relieved of my duties and expelled from the clan if someone knew that I was speaking to you right now." He took a deep breath and I heard him blow it out a few seconds later.

"I'm sorry I called, Kain. I don't want to make things any worse for you."

"They can't really get much worse now, Eviana." His tone was cold and harsh. It saddened me that my actions had turned this caring, virtuous man into the hateful creature on the other end of the line. "What are you calling for anyway?"

My heart was torn. Brendan was lying in the other room, fighting for his life as it dwindled away each day like a leaking bucket. But Kain hated me and it wasn't right for me to ask him to help save my boyfriend.

"Eviana, what do you want?" he asked more loudly but with a slightly softer attitude.

"Brendan's sick and we need your help," I blurted out. Kain laughed deep and strong, but the sound froze the blood in my veins and nearly stopped the beating of my heart.

"Wow, you have some nerve. Asking me to help your *boyfriend*? Are you crazy or just that inconsiderate?"

I knew that I should have been humble and apologetic, but my emotions snapped at that point.

"Okay! I get it! I am the most horrible person in the world and believe me when I tell you that I truly feel that way some days. But I made my choice and we all have to live with it." I continued before he could reply. "I called you because Brendan thinks that a clan leader is controlling the selkies. We were attacked the other night. They stole his skin and I need to get it back. He thought that maybe you would know more about what's going on since you are a leader now, but forget it. Just forget it! I'm sorry that I called!" My hands were shaking and I belatedly realized that I was standing up hunched over the phone, yelling into it like that would help to get my point across.

"Eviana, stop screaming," Kain said with more command in those words than if he would have yelled them. "Start from the beginning and tell me what happened." His sudden change in attitude caught me off guard.

"What?"

"Just take a breath and tell me exactly what happened." He was suddenly Kain Matthew the Leader, and all semblances of hurt feelings and angry attitudes disappeared.

I slunk back down to the floor and told him everything from the beginning of that horrible night up until my phone call to him. He only asked a few questions, but I think that was because he had a hard time understanding me through my sobs and snotty nose. I wiped at my face and took a few calming breaths.

"Have you ever heard anything like this before?" I asked.

"Yes."

When he didn't elaborate I continued. "Mermaid's can do that? We can control other beings?"

"Some can, yes."

"And do you know anyone on the east coast who is strong enough to build an army of selkies?"

"Possibly." I started to get irritated with his short answers, but he spoke again before I could complain. "Give me your address."

"Why?"

"Because we're coming there," he stated. I told him where we were staying and he said to keep the phone close by and to expect them in a day. He hung up before I realized that he said 'we' and 'us' as though he wasn't the only one coming to our rescue. Who could he possibly be referring to?

I had been shunned, which by merfolk standards, was pretty much the worst thing that could happen next to death. Everyone was to act like I was dead, like I never even existed. Kain was taking a big risk for me and the guilt I'd been carrying for so long roared to life again. He was putting everything on the line to help us. Or was he? Perhaps there was more going on in the political underworld than anyone had ever let me know, and maybe this was all part of the bigger issues Kain had mentioned at his appointment ceremony.

But as I sat there and over analyzed our conversation, I realized that I wasn't being totally fair. Although I'm sure that Kain would have some understanding about the political tension and know whether or not these events were connected, he was still coming to see me at great risk to himself and his career. Plus, whoever was coming with him would know that they could be excommunicated from their clan as well.

I climbed into bed next to Brendan and cried. I had abandoned everyone who had been good to me, and now at least one of them was coming to my rescue. I didn't deserve that, but Brendan did and regardless of how tough this was going to be for me, I vowed to do everything I could to save him. Even if that meant dealing with the people who hated me the most.

TWELVE

The knock at the door awakened me from the first bit of sleep I was able to grasp over the past twenty four hours. Wiping my eyes and running my fingers through my hair, I rolled out of the bed to greet my guests. Brendan hadn't moved so I tried to walk quietly and quickly even though the fear of seeing Kain slithered through my bones.

I opened the door to see one stern face and two unexpected companions standing just behind it. Kain's height blocked the rising sun from my view but his dark, ominous silhouette trapped the words in my throat. His expression was blank yet cold, reminding me of something dangerous and on edge. He wasn't happy to be here and he was making no attempt to ease my discomfort. I looked up at him and tried to smile. When I was met with an unemotional stare, I peeked around his shoulder to welcome the two others instead.

Daniel pushed his way past Kain and gave me a hug that nearly caused me to cry. He kissed my check and stepped away, glancing over his shoulder to address Kain. "I can give her a hug," he chided as if he needed to justify some unspoken rule. Turning back to me, he said, "Where's Brendan?"

Wordlessly, I stepped aside and waved my hand toward the bed. Daniel promptly entered our hotel room, threw his bag on the kitchen table, and walked to the injured selkie. He knelt down on the floor and had a whispered conversation with Brendan who had just woken up. I was curious to know what they were talking about, but a nudge against my shoulder drew my attention to the other familiar face.

"So, this was your plan?" Carissa's sultry voice and crooked grin only added intrigue to her persona. Kain snapped his head around to glare at her.

"You knew about this?" he asked. His body shook with anger and if I was on the receiving end of that rage, I would have wilted away.

But Carissa ignored him and stepped toward me. She kissed me on both cheeks like a European and flipped her sunglasses up to the top of her head. Looking around our modest home through the half opened door, I could see her taking in all the flaws and I suddenly felt very uncomfortable. She made a noise of either content or disgust before stepping back away from Kain and me to resume her aura of nonchalance.

"Daniel is going to stay here and we're going for a drive," Kain broke the tense silence. I wanted to make some kind of mafia joke but it wasn't appropriate in this situation. After all, with the way Kain felt about me right now, maybe he did want to "take me on a drive" to make me "swim with the fishes".

"Who's going?" I asked quietly.

"We are," Kain replied nodding his head toward me and Carissa.

"Where are we going?"

"To see someone." All of the fun and life that made Kain such an amazing person had disappeared. I knew I had contributed to that and it troubled me more than I wanted to admit. Behind that hardened exterior, he was hurting. His father was gone, he was a young leader, and worse than anything, I had betrayed him. "Eviana?" I must have been staring at him.

"I-I'll go get dressed. Do you want to come in?" Carissa turned toward the door, but Kain stopped her in her tracks.

"No. We'll wait here." It was such a cold, hard response. I quickly turned around and ran inside before he could see the tears running down my face. Slamming the door shut a little harder than necessary, I slumped against the frame as though it could absorb all of the pain and remorse consuming my body right now.

"Just give him some time," Daniel said from the other side of the room. I belatedly noticed Brendan staring at me with concern and curiosity in his eyes and before I said something to make things worse, I ducked into the bathroom like a coward.

The boys continued to speak in hushed voices and after a few minutes I heard Daniel banging around in the kitchen, presumably finding something for breakfast. Not knowing how I felt about leaving Brendan and Daniel together, I brushed my teeth and hair concentrating instead on making myself presentable.

Brendan was standing outside the door when I opened it, startling a small scream from my lips. "Why are you out of bed?"

Without answering, he pushed me back inside the bathroom, closing the door behind us. In the tiny room we were nearly pressed up against each other and I could see just how horrible he looked. I rested my hand on the side of his cheek to feel his overly warm skin pressing back. "Brendan," I whispered.

He pulled my hand away from his face and smiled at me. "Thank you." Kissing my forehead, he allowed me to wrap my arms around his waist even though I was sure that it hurt him. "I know what this took for you. Just try to focus on the task at hand and let your friends come to you when they're ready." It was probably the best advice anyone could give me and it was exactly what I needed to hear.

I helped Brendan back to the bed just as Daniel walked over with two bowls of oatmeal for each of them. I thanked my friend who didn't seem to hate me at all and joined the two outside that I wasn't so sure about.

The sun escaped its nighttime prison highlighting the sky in brilliant reds and oranges. I briefly recalled the old saying about red mornings and sailor's warnings, and considering the company I was keeping, perhaps I needed to heed the omen.

Following my two silent companions toward the parking lot I wondered what I had really asked for when I called Kain. I knew that there was more going on in the merfolk politics than anyone ever let me know, and now we may be getting ourselves right into the middle of it. But then I thought of Brendan and they way he looked right now and there was no question in my mind that I was doing the right thing.

At the far end of the parking lot was a black Lexus sedan with dark tinted windows and a sleek body design. I stopped to look up at Kain, but Carissa answered my silent question instead. "One of the perks to being in charge."

"This is yours, Kain?" He extended his arm and I heard the beep that unlocked the doors. There was another sound and the car suddenly started while we were still ten feet or more away. Kain never did answer my question but I saw the slight smile that he was trying to hide from me. Maybe there was still some life left in him after all.

We were all in the car heading south along the coast before I finally spoke again. Kain drove and Carissa was in the passenger seat, leaving me alone in the back like a criminal.

"Who are we going to see?" I asked. Carissa turned to look at Kain, but when he stayed silent she resumed her pretend fascination with the scenery outside. "Hello. Is anyone going to speak to me?"

"Jeremiah Williams," Kain finally answered.

"What?" Jeremiah Williams was a legend amongst the merfolk, but more importantly, I thought that he was dead. I said as much to my disgruntled car mates.

"He's very much alive although he would prefer to stay off the radar," Carissa added.

"How do you know him?" I asked directing my question to Kain.

He shifted uncomfortably in his seat and seemed hesitant to tell me. "He's a distant relative."

"You're related to Jeremiah Williams?" The questionable merman had been a famous actor in his younger years, but once he retired from the spotlight the rest of the clans acted like he didn't exist anymore. I'd always wondered if he'd been shunned, although until recently, I didn't think that was a punishment practiced nowadays. The more I thought about it, the more I had a feeling that is exactly what had happened to him. "What did he do?" I asked in a barely audible whisper.

"I don't know," Kain replied solemnly.

Instead of asking anymore questions, I sat back in my seat and thought about what was happening. We were going to see a merman who had done something bad enough to be shunned from the community. Granted, I was also facing the same kind of treatment, but something in my gut was telling me that Jeremiah's punishment was for a far worse crime than being a runaway bride.

We drove for another half hour along the barren Maryland shores, passing a car only every few minutes. The white dunes trimmed with green grasses and the occasional scrub pine, reminded me of the trees that surrounding the lake where Brendan and I met the naiad. I almost wanted to ask if either Carissa or Kain had ever seen a naiad before, but decided to keep that to myself for now.

We pulled into sand driveway leading up to a large beach house. Three white columns held up the aluminum roof of the plantation-like brick home. Lush green landscape bordered the perimeter of the acreage even though the surrounding environment was full of sand dunes. The driveway gates were open as though we were expected and Kain parked the car beside an impressive water feature consuming the majority of the front yard. The fountain masterpiece boasted three different ponds interlaced and connected to a raised structure in the middle. Water spewed from the highest fountain and trickled over the faux rocks and lily pads supplying a constant rhythmic beat of drips and splashes.

Carissa and I admired the gorgeous pink flower at the edge of one of the lower ponds when the water before us suddenly shot up toward the sky, sending droplets raining down all over us.

"And who do we 'ave here?" A strangled accented voice asked. It was as though he was speaking through a tunnel.

I looked up to see a man made completely out of water standing before us. Well, standing wasn't exactly accurate. It was more like he was floating on the water's surface, yet he never broke contact with the pond.

"Aye…cat got yer tongue young maidens?" The accent sounded Scottish and it was somewhat difficult to understand. He laughed and twirled around the pond, reminding me of those captive dolphin shows humans get such a kick out of. Although he never added color to his appearance like the naiad had done, I could see the outline of a hat and jacket on the body of this water sprite. At least I had decided that he must be a water sprite.

"There ye go lassie. I am, indeed, a water sprite." Apparently he could hear my thoughts too. In an instant, his face was abruptly next to mine and I could feel the cool moisture of his aquatic body dripping in front of me. "Abhainn is ma name 'n I am here to serve ye."

I couldn't help but hear the underlying anger in his words and it instantly put me on alert. "It's nice to meet you Abhainn. I am Eviana and this is Carissa and Kain," I said pointing my thumb toward the silent mermaids beside me. Apparently they never saw a water sprite before. "Why would you be taking care of us?" I asked, trying not to sound too ignorant or rude.

Abhainn tilted his head to the side like a vulture and continued to stare at me, probably probing my head to see if I was being sincere with my line of questioning. "Why, that is the way things are, my maiden." When I looked at him in confusion, he straightened up, crossed his arms over his chest and continued. "My master keeps me here to invite in the welcomed guests 'n chase those away who mean harm."

He stunned us all into silence with that explanation. "Do you mean to say that you are trapped here? In this fountain?" Carissa asked with such sincerity in her tone that I turned to look at her in astonishment.

"Aye," Abhainn replied curtly and nodded toward the house. "*He* captured me years ago 'n now I live here," he spread his arms out wide as a wicked grin appeared on his liquid face, "in this beautiful concrete prison." Abhainn laughed again, this time sending chills down my spine.

Turning to face Kain on my right, I whispered, "What has Jeremiah done?"

"I don't know," he murmured back. "Let's go find out."

We turned to walk to the front door, all the while hearing Abhainn swirl around his small watery home in what must have been frustration and resentment. I'd never heard any stories about water sprites being captured before probably because I didn't know they still existed. Yet here it was, in less than a month I had met two. One who was petrified of me and one who had been trapped by a merman. I didn't know exactly what was going to happen next, but I had a feeling that we would leave here with a different view of our kind.

A human servant met us at the door and without saying a word, ushered us inside. The immaculate house had high open ceilings and dark hardwood floors. It smelled of vanilla and something else that I couldn't quite place. We didn't have a chance to notice much more of the architecture since the human man moved through the house without slowing down.

We walked to the back of the living space and I could see that the hallway opened up at the end of our path. Sure enough, the thick humid air hit us like a wall the moment we stepped through the arched entryway into an atrium of sorts. In front of us was a large, rectangular indoor swimming pool complete with rock boulders, waterfalls, and colorful lighting. Around the perimeter sat at least a dozen people with another ten or more standing at attention in various parts of the room.

It took me a moment to realize that something was off with this picture. Every person seemed to be in some kind of trance, or at least that would be the best way to describe it. They hardly moved when we arrived and it made me leery of the merman we were here to meet. An exotic music mix of drumming and chanting filled the background and I belatedly noticed that the pool lights seemed to change colors in sync with the beat of the song.

Our human escort walked to the far end of the pool and bent down next to the edge like he was searching for something in the water. The three of us stood absolutely still at the entrance not knowing what was coming next.

A rustling in the corner closest to us briefly drew my eyes to the side. There, a man around thirty years old, sat on a small wooden stool and stared intently at me. His short black hair was cropped close to his head like a soldier and his dark body glistened with moisture that clung to him like a second skin. Something about him immediately felt familiar and when I caught his scent, my heart nearly stopped beating. It took an immense amount of control not to alert my companions that I had just recognized another selkie.

Considering that we had been attacked only a few nights ago, my first reaction to seeing him in a merman's home was one of fear. Was he being controlled too? Was he one of the seals that had attacked us? An almost unnoticeable smile threatened to escape his lips, but it wasn't malevolent or threatening. He simply seemed to be greeting me without attracting any attention.

"Well, well. My long lost cousin returns at last."

I thought it was a disembodied voice until I stepped to the side of Kain to see the merman swimming in the pool. Jeremiah Williams had to be at least fifty years old by now, but he didn't look a day over twenty. His long blond hair hung freely around face, clinging to his wet neck and carelessly flowing around his shoulders in the water. The strong jaw line and chiseled muscles made him way more beautiful than any man should ever be. It was easy to see why he had succeeded in Hollywood, and it was equally easy to see that he made no attempt to appease anyone but himself.

"Kain, you've let me down." Jeremiah swam over to the edge of the pool and crossed his perfectly toned arms on the edge while shaking his head in disgust. "Look at you! You have the face of an ancient."

"Some of us can't be a playboy all of the time. I have many responsibilities now," Kain replied through gritted teeth.

Jeremiah waved his hand at him. "Nonsense. You have people helping you. Just tell them to take better care of you. We aren't going to stay young forever." His smile creeped me out and I wanted to make a comment about his age, but when I made a small move to step forward, Kain discretely shook his head.

"You have no idea what I face now, Jeremiah," Kain said slowly.

"No?" The merman kicked his tail and pulled himself up on the edge of the pool. Immediately, three female servants ran to his side. One had a towel that she used to gently blot the water droplets off his muscular chest and stomach. The other carried an ornate glass pitcher that she quickly began dipping it in the pool and pouring the contents over the iridescent tail of the merman. Keeping that area wet would allow him to maintain his half human, half fish form for a little longer. The last servant passed a gold goblet to Jeremiah and he took a long sip of its contents before continuing. It was clear that he was putting on a show, and I didn't think it was only for our benefit. Jeremiah liked to perform. "Well, do enlighten me cousin. What is going on that I don't know about?"

Kain sucked in a breath and the next four words he spoke not only changed the entire atmosphere but also promised to have a profound impact on our lives. "We are at war."

THIRTEEN

"What?" Carissa, Jeremiah, and I asked in unison. It was hard to comprehend exactly what Kain meant, especially considering that what he was saying was completely outrageous. There hadn't been a war amongst the merfolk in over a thousand years, and even then that uprising had been squashed relatively quickly and quietly. I couldn't remember what it had been about exactly, but whatever it was, the Council had resolved the matter. Ignoring Carissa and I, Kain took a step closer to his distant relative and addressed him directly.

"The Sutherland clan has declared war on those who will not side with their views to follow The Legacy."

Jeremiah relaxed his shoulders slightly and shrugged. "Oh they've been threatening to do that for years. I'm sure that this is just another political ploy and scare tactic." The gorgeous merman touched each of the girls one at a time on the shoulder and they promptly returned to their positions along the wall. He didn't seem too concerned with Kain's declaration.

"They have already attacked us both here and at home." My head whipped over to look at Kain as I stepped up beside him.

"They've been to our home? What happened? Why didn't you tell me?" Frantic and paranoid, I worried that something terrible happened to our families since I'd been gone.

"It is not your home anymore, Eviana," Kain snapped at me.

It was a slap in the face which only felt worse because there was an audience watching our every move. I knew that I had left my home behind but it didn't mean that I'd stopped caring for everyone there. If something bad had happened, I needed to know.

"Ah," cooed Jeremiah. "So you're the runaway bride." He looked me up and down, assessing every part of my body which was easy to do since I jumped to attention when he recognized me. In the distant corner, I heard the selkie shift on his chair again as though this news was important to him too. Jeremiah slowly shook his head from side to side and made a sucking sound with his mouth. "You shouldn't have let her get away from you, Kain. She would have been perfect."

I expected Kain to set him straight, and when he didn't, I wanted to explain that it wasn't Kain's fault. However, he spoke up before I had a chance. "Jeremiah, they have killed two leaders and are using selkies to do their dirty work. Eviana was attacked just up the coast the other night by three of them. Do you know anything about this?" His tone was brutal. This wasn't a question, this was an accusation.

"Don't you dare!" Jeremiah's tail had transformed back into legs and he pushed himself to standing so that he was eye to eye with his clan leader. "Are you questioning my loyalty, Kain?"

"Do I have a reason to?"

Jeremiah threw his head back and laughed. "Of course you do! Our family shunned me from their world because I refused to stop using my gifts. In fact, following The Legacy wouldn't be such a bad idea." He ran his hands through his hair and smiled. "We are a superior race and we would have continued to rule had the Council not decided to ban the practice of Legacy. Look around this room! Humans and shifters and water sprites are at our mercy. We can control them, so why should we not?"

Kain quickly grabbed Jeremiah by the shoulders and pulled him close enough for a kiss. Through clenched teeth and a shaky voice, Kain ask him the most important question yet. "Are you involved with this, Jeremiah?"

The room was silent with not even a breath being shared amongst each other. We all knew that Jeremiah's answer would change the course of action for the rest of the meeting and right now, Kain seemed determined to do whatever he could to protect his people. Seemingly unaffected by Kain's outburst, Jeremiah looked at his cousin's hands on his arms and then arched an eyebrow in his direction. Kain interpreted the meaning and stepped away slightly.

"No. I am not involved in this war."

Jeremiah held out his arms to the side and another female servant rushed over to wrap a sarong around his waist. The dark red material contrasted greatly with the nude color wraps on everyone else in the room.

Looking around for the first time, I noticed that all of Jeremiah's guests or servants were wearing what looked like ancient Greek clothing. The women wore dresses that wrapped around only the modest parts of their body, exposing the skin on their stomach, arms, and legs. The men had on togas, again draped distinctly to show copious amounts of bare skin without compromising their dignity. Jeremiah had created his own little empire.

"Please, come with me," he continued and waved us over to the corner of the swimming pool area where a simple wooden table and chairs sat. Jeremiah took the end seat at the head of the table, while the three of us gathered along the side. Once again, he was instantly surrounding by the awaiting servants carrying trays of fruit and drinks for all of us. He never said a word to them, and that continued to bother me as I tried to figure out how it was possible. "Cousin, tell me what you know."

"We think that the Sutherland clan has formed a sort of coalition with a few other families both here and in Europe. They want to step out of the shadows and claim their birthright as the ruler of humans and they are willing to take their war public. The Council has been working diligently for the past few months to negotiate terms with the clans and to keep the casualties out of the media spotlight."

I sat and stared at my childhood friend. I had no idea this was going on around me and although I was angry at myself for being so ignorant, I was also angry at Kain and my mother for not enlightening me. Maybe if I would have known the gravity of the situation, I would have made a different choice for my future. Maybe.

"You said that two leaders have been killed. Who were they?" Jeremiah asked.

"One was from a Washington clan, Master Harrison. And the other…"

"Was my uncle," Carissa interrupted. "Ren Kiyomizu. He was killed in his mountain home in the Catskills two weeks ago. It was ruled a natural death, but there were signs that water sprites had been involved."

Jeremiah's eyebrows arched higher than I would have thought possible. "Water sprites, huh?" He rubbed his chin in a way that made me think he once maintained a beard. "You are Carissa Nakamo?" She nodded her head and smiled slightly. "I have seen your work. Very impressive. We should talk more about your future." Kain cleared his throat to remind Jeremiah that there were more pressing issues right now. "Yes cousin, later. I know." He turned to look directly at me. "Tell me about the attack."

Considering that I hadn't spoken more than a few words since we arrived, I looked at Kain to see what he thought. He gave me a small and nearly invisible head bob encouraging me to tell my story. So I spent the next few minutes telling Jeremiah and the servants all about the attack on Brendan and me and how that led up to our visit today.

"They stole his skin?" a deep voice from the far side of the room questioned. As one, we turned to see the mysterious speaker and I was surprised to find that the selkie from the corner stool had started moving closer toward us.

"Malcolm..." Jeremiah warned and the man stopped dead in his tracks.

Kain looked at the merman. "Who is he?"

"He's a selkie," I replied, never letting my eyes fall from the shifter. I felt Kain and Carissa's stare boring into my back, but I could discuss this with them another time. "Why would they take Brendan's skin?" I continued.

Malcolm shook his head and let his gaze drop to the floor. "I-I don't know. If the mermaid clans are controlling selkies, I would think that they would have captured your friend to use him in their army instead. But taking the skin only means that they are ensuring he will have a slow and painful death." He shuddered with those words. "It's just cruel."

"Unless they are using it as bait to bring you to them," Jeremiah added.

"What would they possibly want with me? I have no power and no authority over anyone."

Jeremiah's eyebrows lifted again with that comment but he quickly continued with his thought. "You are the key to the Matthew and Dumahl Clans. If they can't get their hands on Kain or your mother, you would be the next best thing."

"I've been shunned! Our clans would care less if something happened to me."

"Obviously that isn't true, Eviana," he said while acknowledging Kain and Carissa's presence.

Was he right? Even though I'd received nothing but a cold shoulder from Kain, he was jeopardizing a lot to come here and help me. Carissa may have had a more personal reason, but she was still risking banishment as well.

"Malcolm, come!" Jeremiah demanded, pulling me from my thoughts.

As though he lost all ability to think for himself, Malcolm walked closer to the table and knelt down next to Jeremiah's legs. The merman began stroking Malcolm's short hair like one would pet a dog. "Tell me selkie, have you felt a comand?"

"Yes," he replied robotically.

"When?"

"Almost every night, master. It is not strong enough to obey, but it is strong."

"Why is he calling you master?" I asked, realizing that I was standing now to get a better view of this display. I was also quite uncomfortable and didn't care that Kain was commanding me with his eyes to sit down and shut up.

"Because he is mine," Jeremiah replied as though the answer was obvious. "They all are." He looked around the room and I followed his head as each and every servant stared back. "Do you not control your selkie?"

"No!" I gasped. "Why would I do that?"

"Why not?" he asked in return.

"Because it's wrong! Besides, I can't do that. I'm not a leader."

Jeremiah's wicked laugh echoed through the atrium again. "A leader? You don't have to be a leader to control those that belong to us. Who told you such fairy tales?"

I didn't answer. Brendan had told me about the stories of mermaids controlling his kind. He was also the one who said that I couldn't do that to him now.

Malcolm was still sitting next to Jeremiah looking up at the merman like a begging dog. It broke my heart to see this happening in front of me. I would never do that to Brendan, it wasn't fair.

"Are you controlling the humans too?" I asked in a whisper.

"Of course," he scoffed like it was the most idiotic question ever asked. "Humans are the easiest. We've been in control of their minds for thousands of years. Don't you recall your ancient Greek history? Poseidon and Amphitrite? They were some of the first mermaids to interact with the humans and shape their culture. 'Gods of the Sea' they used to call us. Humans would sacrifice each other and their beloved belongings to beg for calm seas and victories in battle. They are so susceptible to superstitions and legends." He laughed and shook his head again. "It is actually quite sad to see how weak minded they are. It really would be a better world if we were allowed to practice The Legacy," he said in a wistful tone.

"Humans are not here to serve us!" yelled Kain.

"No?" Jeremiah snapped. "Then why can I do this?" In an instant, every human servant stood and briskly walked over to the edge of the pool. As one, they jumped in and disappeared underneath the surface.

The stillness was startling after the echoes of the splashes disappeared into the walls. The music beat rhythmically in the background and we all sat in stunned silence. None of the humans came up for air.

"What are you doing?" Kain asked in desperation.

"Proving my point, cousin. If humans weren't around to serve us, I wouldn't be able to enter their mind and tell them to sit on the bottom of this pool until I commanded differently. They will stay there until their lungs give out and they take that last deadly breath. And they will do that simply because I told them to."

"Stop this!" I cried. Carissa and I rushed over to the edge of the pool only to see about twenty bodies sitting on the bottom of their deadly liquid crypt. A few of them began to twitch and release bubbles from their mouths. They were running out of air and Jeremiah was willing to let them die to prove a point. "We get it okay? Humans are weak and feeble. Now please release them!" I screamed at Jeremiah.

"Not just yet," he murmured.

More bodies began to jerk and shudder under the water. Carissa reached down toward one particularly young female who was directly below us, but before her hand got to the water's surface, another one reached up and grabbed her. She let out a scream as a clawed liquid hand with long, bony fingers wrapped around her wrist and held her arm in place.

"What is that?" she cried out.

Shaking her arm back and forth, she tried to dislodge the hand. When she lifted her hand up, an arm, shoulder and then head appeared at the surface as though she had pulled this creature from the depths of its lair. Its hand was large but the rest of the body only seemed to be about three feet long. The water sprite smiled and a mouth full of sharp, pointy teeth filled its malevolent grin. He snapped at Carissa, causing her to scream again.

I heard several noises at the surface of the water like dolphins breaking through for a quick breath, and when I surveyed the pool, I saw at least a dozen water sprites grinning back at us. Each one had an oval shaped head, long pointed ears, and sharp teeth peeking out from underneath their lips.

Yet that couldn't distract me from the real horror. Every human under the water was now struggling. A few of them stopped moving and I feared the worst.

"Please…" I whispered.

As if on command, the water sprites dove under the surface and began to toss the humans one by one up on the side of the pool. Some of them hit the edge hard enough to make a sickening crunch, making me wonder if the sprites were causing more damage. Coughing and sputtering noises consumed the room while the servants began to expel the water from their lungs and breathe in the oxygen they desperately needed.

"What have you done?" Kain gasped as he watched the water sprites play with shoes and pieces of clothes they stole from the helpless humans.

"Who them?" Jeremiah asked innocently as he watched the faerie-like creatures play while he continued to pet Malcolm who hadn't moved from his position. "I own them too. I captured two of them in a bog several years ago and they have bred like bunnies ever since. As you can see, I now have a little family that continues to grow each year. In fact, we are expecting a new arrival in a few weeks."

"This is why they shunned you," I guessed while helping Carissa to her feet. We walked over to Kain who stood on the opposite side of the table as Jeremiah. We had overstayed our welcome and I could see that we were all ready to go.

"For this and other things," Jeremiah replied lightly. "As I said, what's the point of being a merman if we don't use our gifts? You have them too, you know." He waved his hand at each of us. "All of you do. You should try it. It's addicting," he hissed. My body ran cold and Carissa grabbed my hand in hers.

"Are you going to help us?" Kain said stoically.

Jeremiah sighed and turned his attention to the selkie at his feet. "Malcolm," he started like someone would speak to a child. "Do you know where they may have taken the skin?"

Malcolm stirred and tilted his head like he was trying to concentrate. "Maybe," he whispered. "There's a rumor that a large group of selkies has been seen just outside the city. Perhaps this is the army controlled by the Sutherland leader?"

"What city?" I asked.

"Malcolm, what city?" Jeremiah repeated since he seemed to be the only one Malcolm could listen to.

"Baltimore."

"Thank you, shifter." Jeremiah pushed against the selkie to stand up and Malcolm fell back against the floor. The action was so condescending that I almost couldn't stop myself from running over to Malcolm to see if he was all right. But I held my ground for fear of making the situation any worse for Jeremiah's slaves. "If you would like the assistance of my selkie, you may take him."

I looked at Kain who seemed to be contemplating the same scenarios. If we took him then he could get away from here, but

Jeremiah would probably only force him back and punish him. Or worse, the Sutherland clan may call to him and he would be compelled to kill us. I looked over at Malcolm who was staring intently at me. There was a special place in my heart for selkies and this was breaking that home into pieces.

"No thank you," Kain finally answered. He lifted his head and straightened his shoulders. "We will see ourselves out."

Not only did we want to walk out on our own free will, but all of his human servants were still lying around the edge of the pool recovering from their near drowning episode. We turned and began to move toward the arched exit that would get us away from this place.

"Don't be strangers," Jeremiah called after us, making no attempt to stop our hasty retreat.

We gathered the information we needed and Jeremiah succeeded in scaring all of us with his sideshow acts. No one said a word. Only the sound of our shoes clicking against the wood floors echoed through the empty house. I kept feeling that something was watching us around every doorway and behind us in the hall, but I refused to turn around. I didn't really want to know what was there. I had seen enough horror for one day.

FOURTEEN

When we finally made it outside to the front porch, Abhainn was waiting for us in his fountain. "What was going on in there?" he asked in a thick accent. "I could feel the pull of my master 'n it almost made me leave ma pond."

"Could you have done that?" I asked.

"I don't know," he said while shaking his head. "It wouldn't 'ave been smart though. I can't survive very long away from my water." He floated on the water's surface as he followed our movement along the edge of the fountain. "Why are ye leavin' so soon? Did my master scare ye away?"

"Something like that," I grumbled. We reached the car and Kain started it before unlocking the doors.

"Please take me with ye mermaid. I can be of great assistance, 'n this place is not right for me." He fell to his knees at the edge of the concrete border and held his hands together to emphasize his pleading.

"Where are you from?" I asked.

He stood and straightened out a jacket that was barely visible in the outline of his aqueous body. "I come from the Old World, but I was captured in a Canadian lake nearly twenty years ago. This pond," he said as he acknowledged the small watery prison, "is not enough space for me. I am dying and my master refuses to release me."

I looked across the top of the car toward my two companions. After what we'd seen today, I knew that I would never forgive myself for not helping all of these water creatures Jeremiah was keeping captive. And from the identical looks on Kain and Carissa's faces, I guessed that they felt the same. Without speaking a word, I nodded to them and walked back toward the Scottish sprite.

"How would we get you out of here?" I asked.

Abhainn's eyes suddenly glowed a sparkling silver and his grin stretched from ear to ear. In it, I could see hundreds of pointy teeth, but I tried not to flinch for fear of being rude.

"Do ye 'ave a bottle?" I ran over to the car and opened the back door. I remembered seeing a few discarded water bottles in the seat so I quickly grabbed one and approached the sprite.

"What do I need to do?"

"Nothin' lassie. Just put it in the water 'n I will climb in."

I looked at the bottle and then at the sprite, and then back at the bottle again. How would he possibly fit inside? Instead of voicing my question, I did as he said and pushed the bottle under the water. Bubbles instantly filled up the space followed by millions of water particles. Abhainn disappeared beneath the surface and for a few moments, I wondered if this would work. Then I felt a rush of energy push its way into the bottle and my hand warmed as the water heated up inside.

I had captured Abhainn.

Briefly, I wondered how Jeremiah had done this so long ago since this only worked because Abhainn was agreeable. I couldn't imagine what it would take to imprison an unwilling sprite.

I pulled the bottle from the water just as Kain told me to hurry up. Twisting on the lid nice and tight, I jogged back over to the car being careful not to shake the contents too much. Once I slid into the back seat, I held the bottle up in front of me, searching for Abhainn. We were on the road heading to my hotel when a tiny face suddenly appeared pressed against the side of the clear plastic. I almost screamed and dropped my new friend, but recovered quickly enough to avoid disaster. Abhainn had shrunk to just a few inches large and I marveled over his ability. He smiled at me and offered a wave with his tiny hand before disappearing again.

"Is he in there?" Carissa asked as she turned around in her seat to face me. I handed her the bottle.

"Yes."

"I can't believe you stole Jeremiah's sprite," Kain said with bemusement.

"What was I supposed to do? Let him stay there trapped under Jeremiah's commands and in his little fountain." I took the bottle back from Carissa and looked out the window. "It's not right."

"No one's arguing with you," Kain replied.

"So what's going to happen now? Can Jeremiah summon him back?" I asked as a knot grew in my stomach. What if he came after us?

"I doubt that," Kain assured me. "He will be mad but he'll probably just go out and collect another. It seems to be his thing."

"And this is what the Sutherland's want? The freedom to control humans, shifters, and other water creatures?"

"It looks that way," Kain sighed.

"So what exactly is The Legacy?" Carissa asked and I was thankful that I didn't have to be the one to do it and expose even more of my ignorance to my friends.

Kain stayed quiet for a little while but finally began to tell us what we were up against. "It's considered to be our birthright. We've had a special relationship with humans since the beginning of time, and usually we are able to coexist without any problems. But ever since they first came to be, we have had a distinct power over a human's mind. Legend says that it was a gift from Poseidon himself. It allowed for our existence without being discovered and as a result we were worshipped as gods.

"As we became more powerful through our control of humans, the shifters and the water fairies saw the importance of siding with us. It was a relationship that strengthened when we discovered we had the ability to call them to us on demand. For years, the shifters and water sprites fought for power and the right not to be controlled, and ultimately our Council declared a truce and promised that no mermaid would ever be permitted to take away their self control in exchange for their silence and their limited interactions with humans."

"So that's why we are all taught that water sprites are extinct?" I interrupted.

"That and because there are so few left. The selkies are allowed to breed as necessary with the humans, but they are expected to maintain a solitary life away from their human mates so that their secret can be maintained. Once the child is born, it is taken away from its human parent to be raised by the selkie one."

I thought about Brendan and his relationship with his dad. That is exactly what had happened to him, and then once Brendan was old enough to be on his own, his father pushed him away. "So now there are merfolk who…what? Who want to control all humans like their personal puppets? I don't really understand what that would accomplish."

"It's not just about controlling their minds. They want to control the power. It would be easy enough for a mermaid to ask a billionaire to donate all of their money to a false charity. Or command the president of a country to approve policies beneficial to the needs of each clan. It's simply too much control for any one family to have. This has happened before in our history, and wars have been fought with their human soldier puppets over land and money and power. With the world in the position it is in today, another war like that would be the end of us all."

"How many clans are involved?" Carissa asked and I was surprised that she didn't know more considering her family had already been dealing with a direct casualty.

"I'm not sure. We think that there are at least three right now and they are all on the east coast. But for some reason their plight is gaining notoriety and there are numerous clans who are contemplating joining them. There is so much unrest in the human world right now that some of the clans feel like our involvement is inevitable and maybe even necessary."

"They think that war amongst our own is the way to achieve their goal?" I asked in disbelief. "Killing mermaids and controlling lesser species is not the way to fix this."

"And what exactly would you do?" Kain asked critically as he looked at me through the rearview mirror.

"Well...I'd certainly squash the Sutherlands first. Take off the head and the rest will follow, right?"

"And what happens when they send an army of selkies and water sprites after you and your family?" he countered.

"Then we use our abilities to take back control and set them free!" I yelled. A smile curved along the corners of Kain's mouth and that made me nearly jump into the front seat to slap it away. "What?" I demanded.

"You're just like your mother."

"What are you talking about?"

"Your mother? You know, the leader of your clan, the one who gave birth to you, the one you ran away from? Your mother wants to do the exact same thing." He was shaking his head in either disbelief or frustration. "She wants to fight back too."

"Well of course she does! Who wouldn't?" When he didn't say anything, I finally understood. "You don't, do you?"

Carissa glared at him and I could almost see him throw up the walls around his emotions. "No, I don't."

"How can you say that? They are *killing* us. How many will have to die?" Carissa was hysterical and I certainly didn't envy Kain at the moment. He sighed again as though he'd had this argument a thousand times.

"No more should die, but going after them directly will only start the war that they want! There has to be a better way."

"Like what? Talking to them?" she screamed.

"Yes, exactly. We should all approach the Council and let them handle it from now on." His voice was soft but something about it seemed unsure.

"The Council is well aware of the situation and they have not done anything to stop this. My uncle was a very powerful figure amongst our kind both here and in Japan and even after his death, the Council continues to be blind. They are choosing not to help just like we should be choosing to fight back!"

Kain couldn't argue with her anymore and I was in complete agreement. Our families needed to do something before this situation got out of control, which considering what we knew already and what we witnessed Jeremiah do, was getting close.

We were almost back to the hotel and before we made the final few turns, I tried to ease the tension with a change in subject. "I'm going after the selkies in Baltimore."

If I had really thought it through, I would have realized this may not have been the best thing to say.

Both Carissa and Kain proceeded to yell at me and tell me how it would be a suicide mission and that I needed to find another solution. But there wasn't anything else for me to do. Brendan was dying and the only way to save him was to recover his skin. I sat there, in the backseat covered with pillows and magazines and pretended to listen to their concerns. One thing was for sure, my friends were back. They may not have wanted to admit it, but they still cared about me and the warmth of that acknowledgment helped give me the courage I knew I would need to save Brendan.

By the time we arrived, both Carissa and Kain made me promise not to do anything stupid right away, so I did just to get them off my back. Daniel was waiting next to the door with a smile on his face although it didn't quite reach his eyes.

I gave him a quick hug and tried to walk inside. He stepped in front of me and put his hand on the door knob. "Daniel, let me in," I demanded.

"You need to know something first," he said without looking me in the eyes. My stomach plummeted to the ground and nausea swept through me like a freight train.

"What happened to him?" I whispered although I could barely hear the words myself.

"Nothing, Eviana. He's just really sick."

"But he was better this morning! He even got out of bed to say goodbye," I challenged.

"I think that's part of the reason why he's not doing well. It drained him pretty bad and after you left, he fell asleep for several hours."

I pushed past Daniel briefly realizing that I would have to apologize later, but right now only one man mattered to me. Brendan was lying on the bed, crumpled in a heap on one side. The fresh bandages indicated that he had bled through the other ones and my suspicions were confirmed when I glanced at the small hotel trash can near the side of the bed. I reached forward to touch his head and gasped at the sight of his skin. He was pale and dehydrated and I would say that his color was bordering on green. I'd only ever seen one person look this bad before and he had died at Cotillion.

Falling to my knees beside the bed, I decided that I would drive to Baltimore tonight. I didn't know exactly how I was going to find them, but I would just have to figure it out. Brendan didn't have much time left.

"Eviana?" Kain called from the doorway. "We're going to get a room here for tonight. Do you want me to bring you something to eat?"

I cleared my throat and wiped the tears away from my eyes before standing to greet him at the door. "No, I'm okay. I don't want to go anywhere right now."

Kain nodded and left the room, closing the door behind him. I had a few hours before dusk and even less time to come up with a plan. My hand suddenly became very warm and I looked down to see the water bottle still in my grip. Abhainn. Maybe he would be able to help me find the selkies.

I set the bottle down on the table and ran to the bathroom to begin filling up the sink. I didn't know much about water sprites since we'd been told that they had disappeared many years ago. Now I had one in an old water bottle that I was getting ready to release into my bathroom. I briefly thought about whether or not I could play mind control games with him if necessary, but quickly discarded that idea and vowed to never think of it again.

When the water finished filling up, I grab Abhainn's plastic home and poured the contents into the sink. I didn't know what to expect so I simply stood there and waited. Right before I decided that I had killed him, his tiny form grew from the white porcelain sink into a foot high sprite.

"Aye, lassie. Thank ye for freein' me. That was a most uncomfortable ride." He continued to brush himself off as his figure emerged from the water and took its appropriate shape. "Couldn't help but overhear, but it seems like ye've got a wee bit of a problem, no?"

I was thankful that I didn't need to repeat everything to the sprite. "Yes, and I have a favor to ask you." He twirled his hand asking me to continue. "Are you able to find people? Well, selkies in particular?"

"The ones that stole the skin?"

"Yes. They might be somewhere on the outskirts of Baltimore. I have to find them. Brendan won't survive much longer, and if I know where I'm going, then I can leave tonight." I sat down on the toilet and looked up at Abhainn's somewhat disturbing fairy face. "Is that even something that your kind can do?"

He tsked at me and waved his hand. "Do? That is one of the things we are so good at." Relief flowed through my body and for the first time in several days, I thought that perhaps we could get out of this mess.

"Okay, so can you do it?"

"Aye."

"Can you do it *now*?" I asked maybe a little too harshly.

"Aye. But once I leave here, I will need to find ye again." I wanted to ask how he was going to leave and then find his way to Baltimore, but my mind was too full of odd scenarios and unexpected events today.

"What if I meet you at the Chesapeake Bay Bridge? Can you get there?"

"Aye, 'n that sounds like a splendid idea." He tilted his head up toward the ceiling and closed his eyes. "I will need a few hours. What time is it now?"

I peeked out into the living room to see the bedside clock and Brendan's dying body next to it. "Just after one."

"All right then. Meet me at the east end of the bridge at eight 'n I will let ye know where to find yer dogs."

"Seals," I corrected.

"Same thing. Now, please send me away." I looked at him in confusion and he pointed to the sink below his feet. "Pull the drain!"

"Oh, okay." I stood and reached toward the metal drain plug behind the faucet. "You're not going to stand me up are you?" I asked.

"Nah. Ye saved me 'n now I will help ye. It is the way of our kind."

"Thank you, Abhainn," I said with all of my feelings at the surface as I pushed down on the drain.

Abhainn tipped his tiny liquid hat toward me and dove into the water off through the septic system. I was hoping that he would be able to make it to the bay, because right now, all of my optimism relied on his success.

Fifteen

I needed to sleep and eat, and not necessarily in that order. As the evening approached, I tried to draft a plan that included finding a way to steal back Brendan's skin without getting caught. I didn't really come up with much. Since I needed to wait on Abhainn for more information, the most I could accomplish was trying to convince Daniel to stay with Brendan while I went out on some secret mission. He was reluctant at first, not because he didn't want to do it, but because I told him that he was not allowed to tell the others. It had been made quite clear that Kain and Carissa wouldn't be spending a bunch of extra time with me, so it shouldn't have been too difficult to understand why Daniel would be the only one invited to my room.

"Why won't you tell me where you're going?" Daniel asked for at least the hundredth time. "I hope that you're not thinking about going after those selkies on your own."

"That would be idiotic," I replied from the bathroom while trying to discretely pack a small bag of extra clothes. I didn't know how long I would be gone, and I wanted to be prepared in case I had to shift.

Daniel made a small noise that led me to think he didn't believe a word that I was saying. It wouldn't matter though. As long as he didn't tell the others, especially Brendan, then maybe I could slip out undetected. I walked past the two boys on the bed and looked at them. Daniel was flipping through the channels and sitting on top of the covers with his ankles crossed while biting his nails. Brendan wasn't moving much at all. He hadn't come out of his sleep for more than a few minutes at a time, and although I hated to leave him, I knew that his strength was quickly running out. There were no other options at this point.

"Okay, I'll be back in a little bit." Daniel looked at me suspiciously and I had to turn my head toward the floor to hide the guilt and my fear. "Thanks again for helping, Daniel. You have no idea how much this means to me."

"Just hurry back, okay?" I smiled at him and quickly left the room.

Dusk was upon us although it seemed that the night had already arrived since the sky was covered with a layer of thick, dark clouds. I silently walked to our car seeing no one else in the parking lot. But just as I unlocked the doors, two mysterious shadows appeared and blocked me in against the driver's side.

"And just where do you think you're going?" Carissa asked.

"I think she's going to try to take on an army of selkies alone," Kain replied.

"Now why would she do such a stupid thing?" Carissa continued.

"Probably because she thinks that there is no other way to handle this situation."

"Oh for God's sake. I'm standing right here!" I snapped. Turning to face them, I leaned against the side of the car and crossed my arms over my chest. "There's nothing you guys can say that will stop me from going."

Kain nodded. "We figured as much." He grabbed the keys out of my hand and held them above his head when I tried to get them back. "You're not going."

I attempted to jump and reach his hand, but he was one step ahead of me. This wasn't happening now. I got so angry that I let out a scream of frustration and pushed against his chest, forcing him to take a few steps back. "I *have* to go. Brendan is dying and this is all my fault!"

"No, you misunderstood. You're not going alone," he corrected. I looked back and forth between the two of them, taking a second to put it together.

"No. You guys can't come." Shaking my head, I began to pace along the length of the car. "I can't let you do that. It's too dangerous."

Kain laughed this time as he pushed past me and opened the driver's side door. "You don't have a choice." He slid in behind the wheel and Carissa jumped in the backseat.

I stood there like a statue in awe of what my friends were doing for me. They had already risked so much, and now they were probably risking their lives for a selkie boy they didn't even know. Kain started the car and waved me inside with an urgent look. Stunned and overwhelmed, I climbed in.

"Where to?" he asked while backing out of the parking spot.

"The Chesapeake Bay Bridge. And we need to be on the east end by eight." He looked at me but didn't ask any more questions. In fact, no one said a word. It took us an hour to get to our destination and almost as long before anyone asked me why we were meeting at this location.

"You flushed Abhainn down the drain?" Carissa asked in dismay.

"It's not like I flushed him down the toilet. It was the bathroom sink and it was his idea." A ball of nerves twisted up in my stomach washing over me in a wave of panic. I really hoped that the water sprite would be here. He was the only semblance of hope I could cling to right now.

"Do you think he can find them?" Kain asked softly.

I turned to look out the window. "I hope so," I whispered.

We finally made it to the beginning of the bridge and instead of paying the toll we pulled off the road and into the visitor's center parking lot. I jumped out of the car and ran toward the first pillar, right where the land ended and the waves fought against their impeding barrier.

I heard Carissa and Kain walk up behind me, although they chose to stay a few feet away. Maybe they were giving me privacy, or maybe they were apprehensive about all of the creatures that we now knew may be waiting under the surface.

"What time is it?" I yelled back to whoever would answer.

"Five after eight," Kain briskly replied.

Great. Abhainn was late and all of the hope I'd been clinging to started to seep from my bones like melting ice. Brendan was going to die and it was because I didn't protect him. I'd relied on him for so much of everything I do, and the one time he needed me, I failed.

My shallow breaths were a sign of an oncoming panic attack, and I tried to control my breathing so I wouldn't lose it in front of my friends. Kain started to walk closer toward me, but I quickly retreated to the water's edge. He didn't need to see me crying.

"Thought I forgot, eh?" a raspy, accented voice called to me. Turning my head quickly, I tried to find the source. "Over here, lassie." In the darkened shadows of one bridge piling stood a lean man in a long trench coat and a bowler's hat. Using the leg propped up against the side, he gracefully pushed away from the structure and glided toward me.

"Abhainn?" I asked. "How…?" If I wouldn't have known any better, I would have passed him off as a mere human. Albeit, an oddly dressed one.

"Ye like?" he asked. With arms spread, he turned in a circle several times, allowing me to take note of his solid and non-aqueous body. "It's been a while since I've been able to do this." He smiled broadly and pulled down on his jacket.

"You creatures can do that?" Carissa tactlessly asked. Abhainn shot her a glare.

"I am no more *creature* than ye. And yes, when we've had our fill, the magic is stronger and more useful." He waved his hand toward the closing visitor center. "I've spent the last half hour wandering amongst those things. Not a one suspected I was anything but a curious tourist."

"What do you mean by having your fill?" Kain questioned. I looked up at his face and noticed suspicion written all over it.

Abhainn's laugh chilled the night air. He slowly sauntered over to us, feigning picking something out of his teeth. With his new body, he was at eye level with Kain but my friend didn't give up any ground. I, on the other hand, unwillingly stepped back at the sudden change in the sprite's demeanor. "I think ye know what I'm referring to, laddie." The two stood in silence, locked in a bitter stare.

Carissa came up behind the other side of Kain and slapped Abhainn lightly on the shoulder. "Well, I don't know what you are talking about, so would you please enlighten us?" She was at least attempting to break the tension.

Abhainn took one step away and looked between Carissa and me several times before he let out a laugh. "Ye really don't know, do ye? What are they teaching ye sirens nowadays? Are we no more than a fairy tale?"

"Abhainn..." I pleaded. "What helps strengthen your magic?"

A wicked grin appeared on his face and for an instance, I thought that I saw his bone structure elongate slightly before flashing back to the non-threatening human façade. "Well, lassie. All we need is a good meal to keep the body strong."

"A meal?"

"He means a human, Eviana." Kain turned his head toward me. "He ate a human."

"Two actually," Abhainn chimed in. I looked at the water sprite with a new sense of disgust and fear. There were stories about the water fairies and their desire to consume human flesh, but we were never told that this was how they survived. Then again, we were told that no more of their kind existed. I thought back to the naiad in the lake and wondered how many human hikers she'd consumed over the years.

"Was that really necessary?" Carissa asked jokingly, although I could hear the nerves fluttering amongst her words.

Abhainn rubbed his hands over his belly and groaned. "I probably could have done without that last one. He was a bit pudgy 'n I fear that I may 'ave over indulged." He was enjoying this way too much. "But alas, I needed my strength. It's been far too long since I've had a decent meal."

I wanted to ask more about this lifestyle. Whether it was fascination or just morbid curiosity, I wanted to know more about him and his kind. But my thoughts were cut short when Kain asked Abhainn what we really needed to know.

"Did you find them?"

"Aye."

"And....?" I prodded after a few seconds of silence. Abhainn sighed and walked to the water's edge. I followed closely behind, with Kain and Carissa staying back where we'd stopped.

"There are seven of them and they are holed up in a dump just outside of the town of Severna Park."

"Did you see them? Do you know if they have Brendan's skin?" Abhainn placed a hand on my shoulder for comfort.

"No, I didn't see them. An...acquaintance reported back to me about their location." I pushed his arm away.

"How do you know that your acquaintance is telling the truth or that they even know who you were looking for?" my high voice screeched. The tightness in my chest came back again and I struggled to breathe.

"I am confident in her assessment. She could identify a selkie from a mile away."

"Did you find them?" Kain asked. He must have heard my panicked cry and decided that he didn't care if this was a private conversation anymore.

I looked at Abhainn again, wondering if I could believe a sprite that ate humans and who outsourced his obligations. "As I was telling your friend, aye. But I don't know if they 'ave the skin or if it is the group being controlled," he continued. "Since yer selkie seems to believe living in a group is rare, than we deduce that this must be the selkies you are looking for."

"Who's 'we'?" Kain asked.

"His *acquaintance*," I snapped. Abhainn looked at me with little patience and much annoyance.

"She is to be trusted," he stated as though that was the end of the conversation. "You will find them at this address." He reached into his pocket and pulled out a tightly folded piece of paper.

However, before we could make the exchange, a horrible noise pulled our attention back over toward Carissa. The ominous crunch of a soft body being beaten and the thump it makes when it falls to the ground was unmistakable.

The bridge lights from above cast an eerie shadow over our meeting place and I could see that Carissa was lying in a heap at the foot of a large man. His silhouette revealed a long object dangling from his hand that appeared to be a bat or baton of some sorts.

"Carissa!" Kain cried and darted toward her. The man that knocked her out raised the bat and pointed it at Kain.

"Not another step or the next hit will meet her skull."

Kain froze and I stepped up beside him. "Did you kill her?" I cried out.

He looked down at Carissa and used his right foot to push her over onto her back. The way her body moved like rag doll caused my stomach to drop. She couldn't be dead. Not this way. Not because of me.

"She'll live," the man stated coolly.

Three more figures made their way into the light. From where we were positioned, tourists and drivers wouldn't be able to see us. The land sloped slightly toward the water, and right now we either ran up the hill past our assailants or used the water as our escape.

"Don't even think of it," a female sneered at me. "We've covered that area as well."

As one, Kain, Abhainn, and I turned toward the bridge and the dark waters splashing underneath. At first I didn't see anything, but when Abhainn inhaled a sharp breath, I followed his gaze to the closest piling.

Twenty tiny heads lifted up at once and began to swim toward us. Their synchronized movement caused a large wave to form, and the sound of the rolling water overshadowed by the cackling and laughing coming from the sharp toothed creatures. Large wings sprouted on a few of the approaching bodies and they took to the air like it was as natural as the need to breathe.

In an instant, our escape to the sea was blocked by six human-like figures. At least as tall as Kain, I couldn't tell if the leathery bodies were male or female. Each one had long hair that hid their slightly slanted eyes, an elongated crooked nose, and fangs that were too large to be concealed. Although they were naked, their bodies were anatomically indistinct from one another. They also smelled. Bad.

"Nixies..." Abhainn whispered in awe. "Where did ye find them?" He reached toward the largest of the group as though he needed to touch it in order to believe it existed. The creature snapped at Abhainn and let out a screech that reminded me of an owl. Or more like that of a mouse being caught by an owl.

"I think she likes you," the man said. "Calypso, you may take him."

In an instant, chaos broke out. Kain ran at the man that had attacked Carissa and I pulled on Abhainn's arms as the nixies tried to drag him back into the water. They seemed to be equally matched and I watched Abhainn fade in and out of existence as he melted into a liquid form, making it difficult for any of the nixies to grab him. As it was quickly evident that Abhainn wasn't incapable of handling himself, I focused my attention back on the fight taking place over top of Carissa's limp body.

"Stop!" I cried out and jumped on the back of a smaller man who had Kain in a choke hold. Without missing a beat, the man threw me off and I landed to the ground with a smack. Immediately, the female selkie was on top of me, straddling my hips and holding my arms down.

"So you're the one he wants?" She cocked her head to the side like a ravenous bird. "What is so special about you?" Grabbing my chin with her hand, she turned my head from side to side as though her answers were hidden somewhere on my face. "You are just a child. Just an ignorant, hideous, ahh…"

She screamed when Kain's foot landed hard in the side of her ribs, almost knocking her off of me. I used her forward momentum to toss her the rest of the way and sent her rolling down the slight hill. Kain pulled me to my feet and looked around. He was breathing heavy and I thought that I saw blood above his eye. Though before I could check, my legs were yanked out from underneath me and I went sprawling to the ground. The air flew from my chest and I saw stars for a few seconds.

At the same time I was incapacitated, the three remaining selkies attacked Kain in unison. He didn't have a chance. Two of them held his arms behind his back while the large man, who seemed to be the leader, punched Kain in the face, ribs, and stomach. The only female of the group pushed her knee into my upper back and yanked on my hair until I was bent as far backward as my body could go.

"You are so weak," she hissed into my ear. "Just like that boyfriend of yours." Each time I struggled, she'd pull on my hair until I was sure that would be ripped out.

Abhainn let out a horrified scream and I turned as much as I could to see that one of the nixies had torn off his arm. There was no blood, since his body was only magically induced, but the sight was still gut-wrenching and apparently the move had caused him pain. I forgot about my own body for a moment and focused instead on what I needed to do to help my friends.

Pulling my arms around to the front of my chest, I launched myself off of the ground while slamming my head back into the female selkie's face. The crack of her nose gave me a trickle of satisfaction and the energy I needed to face off with her. She fell backward onto her butt and covered her nose with both hands, blood pouring out from between her fingers. I smiled, but little did I know that my glory wouldn't last very long.

Upon seeing his companion on the ground, the smallest male let go of Kain and rushed me instead. I barely had a chance to block his fist that he intended to knock me out with. He hit the back of my neck instead but the force was still great enough to cause me to stumble. I fell to my hands and knees and instantly the man was behind me with his arm wrapped tightly around my neck.

From this position, I got my first real look at Kain and I nearly lost all desire to fight for my own life. His eyes were already swollen and blood covered his face. Only one selkie held him now, while the leader landed more punches. When I saw the man raise the bat to take a swing at Kain, something inside of me snapped.

"Stop now!" I yelled.

And when I did, it seemed as if time slowed. Some bundle of energy from deep within me rose to the surface and exploded from my skin. It felt like a million tiny pins pricking me from the inside out, yet the sensation wasn't painful. Energy rolled off of my body leaving it quivering and wanting for more. Something had happened. Something had changed.

I belatedly realized that no one held on to me anymore. The female and male selkies that had attacked me now knelt on the ground and stared at me in awe. Cars continued to rhythmically bang over head as they crossed the pieces of bridge pavement. There were no more fighting noises, no more cries.

I stood on my own and looked at Kain's attackers. The large man had stopped mid-motion with the bat still raised high above his head, readying for a swing. But he no longer looked at me or Kain. Instead, he stared at his minions with his jaw hanging open.

The man behind Kain sat on the ground like the other two selkies and watched me like a lost puppy. Kain fell forward on his hands and knees, wheezing and spitting up blood. When he finally looked at me, I could see a hint of fear on his face.

"Eviana?" he whispered.

That sound was enough to break whatever spell the selkie leader had succumbed to. He lowered the bat and shook his head. Running his hand through his hair, he let out a partial laugh.

"You are strong, but not strong enough." He turned to me and straightened his shoulders. "These ones do not belong to you."

I didn't even have time to interpret his declaration. The man took two giant steps toward me and swung back his arm. I remembered trying to avoid the blow just before I felt the sharp pain from the impact and everything went black.

SIXTEEN

Someone kept hitting me in the face. First on the right check, then the left. Each slap sent a new wave of pain through my head and neck. When I finally opened my eyes, the darkness of the evening blinded me to my surroundings. I could smell a dense forest interspersed with a slight scent of wet animal. Something moved beside me, but when I tried to turn my head in that direction, I got another slap in the face.

"Enough! I'm awake," I yelled.

"It's about time," grumbled a deep voice that I think belonged to the selkie leader from the bridge.

A second later, I was yanked to my feet, the back of my head screaming at me in pain. The force of the hit that knocked me out must have cracked my skull because I was feeling nauseous and weak.

A large pair of arms wrapped around me before I could fall back to the ground. "Move!" he commanded.

I stumbled along a dirt path, tripping over rocks and slipping in the mud. The air was cool but humid, and I sensed water nearby. As if on cue, the distant sound of a rushing waterfall encompassed the evening silence. I popped my head up and toward my left to see if I could find the source, but I saw something much more disturbing instead. "Daniel?"

Sitting against a tree just a few feet in front of me was my friend. His hands were tied around his back and his head hung at an awkward angle. When I yelled for him again, he stirred, moaning as though he couldn't speak.

I tried to run to him, but the selkie still holding on to me jerked my arms back so quickly that the searing pain in my shoulders brought tears to my eyes.

"I'm sorry," Daniel croaked.

I leaned me head backward to try and face my prison guard. "What did you do to him? Where is Brendan?"

If they had Daniel, then they knew where Brendan was. I hoped that he was in this forest with us because the alternative was not something that I could even begin to fathom. The man behind me wouldn't answer and instead continued to push me toward the bank along the river below us.

As I walked past Daniel, the female selkie appeared and I heard her slapping and pushing my friend around. I wanted to do something, but the pain in my skull forced me to focus my efforts on simply not passing out. When we reached the edge of the forest, I saw the waterfall reflecting in the moonlight, and scattered around the large pool were several bodies.

"Ah, she wakes," someone cooed from the water's edge.

My captor pushed me toward the embankment causing me to lose my footing and roll down the rough terrain. Thankfully, my hands weren't bound and I was able to save my head from incurring further damage.

Lying in a crumpled heap, I decided not to move until they made me. The scenery spun and a headache pulsed behind my eyes. I thought that my vision was blurring until my brain interpreted what I was looking at.

"Brendan? No!" A large seal was sprawled out over the rocky beach of the pool, but he didn't seem to be capable of moving much. One of his green eyes rolled up to look at me. The pain in it was evident but what really took my breath away was the look of disappointment. "How did you...?"

"Find him? Change him?" The man standing on the river's edge moved closer to Brendan. He was tall but svelte, with dark hair that hung past his shoulders. His bare chest glistened in the moonlight and his jeans hung loosely on his body. The selkie knelt down and rubbed his hand slowly over my boyfriend's back. "Your hotel key was in the car." He looked up at me and shook his head. "Not too difficult to figure out." Returning his attention back to Brendan he spoke directly to him. "You almost died and I saved you. Now you just need to do one more thing."

Another body rolled down the bank and slammed into me before I could ask any questions. His groan was familiar and I struggled to turn and comfort him too.

Kain's face was still battered and bruised and his hands were tied behind his back like Daniel. A piece of cloth had been shoved in his mouth as a makeshift gag. We looked into each other's eyes for what seemed to be several minutes with hundreds of silent messages passing between us.

My heart was breaking into a million pieces. Every single person in my life right now was in danger, and there was no one to blame except me.

"Do you see that?" The man continued speaking to Brendan. "She will never be yours completely. Our kinds are not meant to mix."

"Who are you?" I snapped, not thinking that he'd give me the courtesy of an answer.

"My name is Julian." He stepped over Brendan and walked closer to me. Bending down, he reached out his hand. I hesitantly grabbed it as he assisted me up off the ground. Being this close to Brendan sent shivers through my spine. He was here physically, but mentally I knew that he was damaged. It would have taken a lot of energy to transition, especially if he was barely conscious. Something remarkable must have occurred between Brendan and Julian. "Your selkie will be fine," he commented upon seeing me look down at my boyfriend.

"How did he change?"

Julian chuckled. "I made him."

"I...I don't understand."

"And you don't need to," he chastised me. "He is no longer yours to worry about." His arm slipped around my shoulder and I did the best I could to dodge his physical contact. Stumbling a few steps away, I turned to face him.

"What do you mean? I love him! He's with me and I'm going to worry about him until the day I die!"

Julian waved his hand in the air. "Yes, well, we will just have to see about that." He walked over to Kain and forcefully pulled him up into a sitting position. "If you want to worry about someone, you should worry about your own kind."

"Leave him alone!" I yelled.

"Oh don't upset yourself, Eviana. My job is to bring him in alive." Julian stood and looked around the water's edge. "All of you."

Confused, I followed his gaze to see Carissa lying several feet away and the female selkie pushing Daniel down the embankment. All of them. All of my friends had been captured.

"What do you want?" I asked.

"My master would like to speak with the lot of you. Apparently you have some very important decisions to make."

I had no idea what he was talking about. The selkies were obviously working together for a clan or clan leader, but what I didn't understand was why a bunch of teenage syrenkas were so important.

Wishing I could talk to Kain and find out more about what was really going on, I found myself walking toward him. He was sitting on his own now, staring up at Julian with a rage I'd never seen from him before. Thankfully the gag in his mouth stopped him from saying whatever was running through his mind.

They moved Daniel to the water's edge next to Carissa. She started to wake up, rubbing the back of her head and wincing with each movement. The two selkie's standing guard began to strip out of their clothes, apparently not too concerned with my friends.

"We all need to change," Julian said. I stared at him. "Come on," he demanded while pulling Kain to his feet. "We don't have much time."

Our remaining captors started poking at each of us. Julian stripped out of his jeans and picked up a seal skin on the far side of the water's edge. I stood there trying to figure out what was going on. Carissa let out a shrill scream and I saw one of the naked selkie's trying to pull off her blouse.

"Stop! What are you doing to her?" I shrieked.

The man looked at me with that same dumbfounded expression I saw under the bridge. Julian's head snapped back and forth between the two of us. He arched his eyebrow and the corner of his mouth turned up in a smirk.

"Sebastian, let her change on her own." Julian spoke to the other selkie, but his gaze never left me.

I watched as Sebastian walked toward a large boulder to retrieve his skin, slip into a seal, and dive into the water. He looked at us once, and then swam below the churning surface and disappeared.

"Where did he go?" I asked.

Julian focused his attention back on Brendan although he still continued to sneak glances my way.

"Under the waterfall. It's where we're all going." With a grunt, he pushed Brendan around so that his head was facing the water. Brendan didn't make any noises, and he didn't try to move by himself.

PROMISES

I started to walk toward them, but Julian held up his hand to stop me. "He is coming with us," he said as though that would be satisfying.

Julian leaned in close to Brendan and whispered something to him. I was just about to protest, when Brendan grunted and pulled himself into the water. Julian noticed me staring at the empty rocks where Brendan had just been and he snapped his fingers at me. "Let's go. All of you."

Julian tossed his skin over his shoulder and began picking up pieces of clothing. Shirts, pants, and shoes were strewn all over the rocky beach like a storm has washed them ashore. Kain pushed up to his feet but stumbled as though it made him dizzy. Daniel did the same and I immediately went over to help untie my friends. I pulled the gag out of Kain's mouth first and watched him cough and sputter until his jaw moved normally again.

When Julian stopped what he was doing, I said, "They can't change like this." He nodded and continued picking up the clothing of his underlings.

"Do you know what's happening?" I whispered to Kain while untying his hands. A small shake of his head was all the answer I got. While I helped Daniel, Kain made his way toward Carissa and helped her undress. It was such an intimate moment between the two of them I had to turn my head so I didn't react. I knew I'd ruined any chance of Kain and me remaining friends, but I guess there was a part of my heart that ached for him to still hold some semblance of a torch for me. Impossible, I know. But I always wanted to be important to him.

Daniel and I struggled to walk into the water. Julian collected all of our clothes and put them into a waterproof bag. One of the selkie minions allowed him to strap the bag to his back before diving head first into the dark waters. My change was forced and painful, but I tried not to show any outward signs of my discomfort. I had to remain strong for my friends.

Carissa and Kain made their way toward the waterfall, followed by Daniel and me. The four remaining selkies, including Julian, pulled on their skins and joined us in the water. One by one they disappeared underneath the surface. The cold water sent shivers through my body, but the fear of what we were going to encounter next chilled me to the bone.

Julian snorted and nodded his head toward the falls. I looked up at the sky and the partial moon and wondered if this was going to be the last time that I would see it. The rushing water sprayed us with a mist and that made me think of Abhainn. Not only were we in trouble, but I didn't know what had happened to him. There was a good chance that after he'd finally found his freedom he had been captured again, or even worse, killed.

A sharp slap on the water forced me to turn around. I saw the final glimpse of a mermaid tail retreating into the water and then it was just Julian and me. I wanted to fight him. I wanted to hurt him for what he was doing. But something was telling me to save my strength because we hadn't seen the worst of it yet. I got another snort accompanied by a flash of sharp canines as the final warning.

Taking my time, I grabbed a long breath and plunged into the unknowing depths below.

SEVENTEEN

The noise from the waterfall dissipated under the surface and after a few feet, the pool became clear. Leaving the churning and tumbling behind, I swam down and down until I could see the bottom. Julian bumped up against my side and nudged me toward the large rock wall that had created the water fall. I was confused until I looked a little closer.

At the base of the outcropping and hidden deep under the rushing water was a cave. All of my friends and the remaining selkies had disappeared, presumably into this tunnel. I swam toward the opening, surprised to see that it was larger than I'd originally thought. Bracing both arms against the entrance, I tried to see through the depth of the cave. However, beyond the first few inches, everything was dark.

I felt another shove against my back and resisted the urge to punch Julian in the face. Instead, I pulled myself forward feeling a bit of satisfaction when my tail slammed against the selkie's body.

The cave was so black that I needed to use my hands to guide me through. Although I could hold my breath for a long time once I transitioned, a little spark of panic tumbled in my stomach. What if I couldn't get air? What if I drowned? But I quickly tried to squash those ridiculous notions. Selkies needed to breathe too, so I doubted that they would lead us into a trap. At least not one that was going to drown us.

The cave seemed to go on forever. I was twisted and turned around curves and boulders, sometimes scraping my body against the sides. After what seemed to be several minutes, I could see a little bit of light ahead. It was just enough to make out the dark rocky walls interspersed with ledges and grooves that showed the history of how this cave had been formed. Millions of years had carved their markings and made a lasting impression on the earth.

The deep, calm interior pool became the welcoming center. When I surfaced, I immediately began searching for my friends only to be disappointed when Julian arrived and I didn't see any of the others. He nodded toward the far side of the pool, expecting me to follow. Instead, I took in my surroundings.

The cave ceiling was now at least a hundred feet high and the entire opening seemed to be as vast as a house. Large flame lanterns hung periodically along the walls, high enough above the water not to be a problem. They cast an eerie glow heightened by the uneven rocky walls enclosing us. Water dripped and dropped from the ceiling, but in the distance, I thought I heard voices.

Wanting to find my friends and get out of here, I hurried to the side of the pool in time to see Julian step from his skin and walk into a darkened area. A large, flat rock provided the perfect structure for a wading beach and as I propped myself up on to it, I turned so that my back faced Julian. I didn't need him observing my change, especially since I suspected that it was going to be painful.

It was. And the more I tried to ignore the sharp breaking and twisting of bones and muscle, the more it hurt. I sat there in utter silence, deciding that now was not the time to show any more weakness. I had already made enough bad decisions that potentially cost my friends their lives, it was the least I could do to try and be strong for them.

I don't know how long I was sitting there before I felt like I could move again. Changing into my human form had always been so easy and welcoming for me. Perhaps it was because of the situation, although I also secretly wondered if something else was happening to me. With everything else going on right now, my capture in particular, I decided not to worry about that at the moment.

"Here," Julian's calm voice cut into my thoughts. "You will need it."

I turned to see that he was holding a blue silk robe in his extended hand. Briefly, I thought that perhaps he was uncomfortable with my nudity, until I saw that he was wearing something similar. Although his robe seemed to be thicker and longer than mine, it was still the same royal blue color which appeared almost black in the limited lamp light.

I grabbed the robe but refused to thank him for it. When I tried to tuck my legs underneath me though, my bones protested to the sudden movement. Apparently, I needed a little more time to recover. I was embarrassed at this and that only made my blood boil more. It was when Julian sat down next to me that I almost lost control. I didn't want to be around him and right now he knew that I couldn't get away. I let out an exaggerated sigh and tried to position my back toward him.

He laughed softly at my childish behavior. "You don't need to hate me so much, Eviana," he cooed.

"What? You kidnapped all of us! Why wouldn't I hate you?" I turned so that I could look at him directly in the eye. "If you hurt Brendan, I swear…"

"You'll what?" he cut me off.

"I'll kill you," I sneered.

Julian looked at me for a few moments without saying anything. I was about to turn away when he snorted and another irritating smirk appeared on his face.

"I think you would, too." He stared off at the distant edge of the pool where we had entered through the underground tunnel. Pulling his knees up to his chest, he hugged himself. It was such an odd movement for someone of his size and age. It almost humanized him for a brief instant.

Speaking to the distance he said, "Our kinds are not supposed to be together. It doesn't ever work out." He shook his head before continuing. "You are going to have to let him go, Eviana. You do not belong together."

There were a thousand things that I wanted to say to him at that moment. Like *it's none of your business* or *he is my soul mate and that it doesn't matter what kind of shifters we were*. But what I said instead surprised even me.

"You've done this before, haven't you?" Something about his slumped shoulders and faraway thoughts led me to believe that he had walked a day in my shoes. He had loved a mermaid once.

This time his laugh was forced and the smile seemed to cause him pain. "Very perceptive." He looked at me. "I am impressed." I blushed at his praise and broke the eye contact. "Yes, I have personal experience with a situation not unlike your own and believe me when I tell you that it won't work out."

"Brendan and I are different," I stated.

"No, you're not."

"Yes, we are," I foolishly argued. "I left my home to be with him. I gave up my responsibilities and my clan because I couldn't bear the thought of living without him. We have grown up together, know each other's deepest secrets, and want nothing more than to be with each other." Julian chuckled again and looked at me with sympathy contorting his face. "What's so funny?"

"Young love." He let go of his knees to stretch out his legs. Crossing one over the other at the ankles, he leaned back and gazed upward like he was watching the stars. "Brendan is a good kid, but he will leave you one day. It is his duty and he will not be able to ignore the call." He was referring to the fact that all selkies had to mate with a human in order to prolong their line. Brendan told me that he didn't want that for himself and I always believed him.

"He won't do that," I countered. Again, Julian glanced my way in pity.

"He will, Eviana. It may not be now, or five years from now. But one day the call will be too much for him. It is the bane of our existence. He won't be able to fight his nature forever."

I was momentarily speechless. Here sat Julian, an older and supposedly wiser selkie telling me that my boyfriend, the only person in this world I wanted to spend the rest of my life with, would someday leave me to impregnate another female. And once that was done, he would stick around until the birth, steal the child and raise it on his own as they all do. Could I handle that? Could I help him raise another women's child? Would I be able to get past that betrayal?

"And it would seem as though you have obligations of your own," Julian continued, bringing me back to the present.

"Huh?" I cleverly replied. Julian smiled.

"You are the next in line amongst the Dumahl clan. I am sure that this entails much responsibility in your future." I couldn't help but laugh.

"Well, I guess you haven't heard then. I've been shunned. No leadership in my future." I watched Julian's face to see if this was news to him. It stayed annoyingly blank.

"That is interesting, but I don't believe it will stop your advancement."

"What are you talking about?" I felt like I've asked that question a zillion times in the past few days.

"You will be a leader, Eviana. There is no denying it. In fact, your powers are already increasing. You cannot be with Brendan."

"My powers?"

"Yes. Your ability to control humans and other shifters?" He looked at my stunned expression and shook his head. "Did they teach you anything?"

I had to join him in laughter. "No, they don't as I've so grudgingly learned the last few days." The first I'd really heard about this mind control stuff was when we met Jeremiah Williams, and I certainly didn't like what I'd discovered.

"But you know about mermaid abilities?" he prodded.

"Yes," I said, even if I didn't fully understand everything. "And I know that they are not supposed to appear until we take leadership. I don't know why that is, exactly, but that's what happens."

"Well, I will tell you that it has nothing to do with leadership." He pointed toward my heart. "It's in there. You are either born with it or not. And you, Eviana, are strong."

He was the first person to ever call me strong. Strong-willed, strong-minded, sure. But not strong in a powerful and useful way. For an instant, I let my mind absorb that compliment to its fullest. If only my mother and father knew that. If only my bratty sister knew what I could supposedly do with my mind, then maybe she would have some respect for me. Or maybe I could force her to.

I thought about Kain and his position now. Would he be able to forgive me if he knew what I could do? I could help him if he needed me and together we would rule our families with strength and power. I could actually become what I was meant to be.

And then I thought about Brendan. He'd been cautioned about mermaids as a child. And now it seemed as though the danger for him was more real than ever. I sighed then picked up a small pebble and tossed it into the water as far as I could. It barely made it halfway, but the ripples distracted me from reality for a while.

"What is it?" Julian asked with sincere interest.

"I was just thinking about something Brendan told me. He said before his father left him that he warned him to stay away from mermaids." I turned to look at Julian. "Apparently he was right." I tried to smile at the irony of it all, but I could barely muster a grin.

"He told you that?" Julian questioned.

"Yes. I think he found it amusing considering that we had already met by then."

"Hmm." He didn't say anything else for a while. I tossed another pebble into the annoyingly calm waters and was surprised when Julian followed my lead. It seemed to be calming for the both of us. Suddenly, I had a thought.

"Can I control you?" That earned me a full out laugh this time.

"You're not that good, Eviana."

"But I think that I did something at the bridge. I think that maybe I controlled some of your selkies."

"They aren't my selkies," he was quick to correct me. "And, yes, I think that your abilities manifested when you were afraid. But it wasn't enough. Not yet." Instead of being fearful of me, he almost seemed…proud. Like he was going to enjoy the day when I would have enough power and control to act as puppet master to all other creatures. "Put your robe on."

"Why?"

"Because they are waiting for us." Julian stood and walked away from me. "Your legs should be good by now."

I wanted to throw a pebble at him for noticing my weakness. But my legs were in fact healed and pain-free, so I stood and wrapped the soft silken robe around my naked body. I noticed that my head wasn't hurting nearly as bad, thanks to my change. Doing a quick assessment of all my injuries, I realized that I felt pretty good considering the situation.

Julian disappeared into the darkness, leaving me alone with the steadily dripping water. I called after him.

"Where did they take Brendan?" My feet slipped on the damp rocks and I tried not to look too uncoordinated as I hustled after Julian.

"He's with the others," his voice echoed off of the barren walls.

"I want to see him," I demanded.

"I'm sure that you do."

It seemed as though our little bonding session was over and it was back to business for the both of us now. I continued to ask, poke, and prod for more information, but it appeared that Julian was finished speaking to me. He didn't seem like an evil minion, but he refused to answer my questions about why he had kidnapped us.

When I finally gave up, I realized that we must have walked nearly half a mile deeper into this never-ending cave. At some point, the rocky ledges gave way to a manicured pathway. The walls of the tunnel had been carved out to allow for more elaborate torches and high ceilings. It was like we were in a castle, with the stone walls and damp interior. But this castle was hidden somewhere far underground. Someplace where no one could find it. Or us.

There was a door up ahead and to the left. It was the first one I had seen and it was made of stone. Impressed, I had to look at it a little bit closer. The thing must have weighed a ton and it was unclear to me how the hinges were set.

"What's in there?" I asked.

Julian stopped in front of the door and began to pull it open. "It's where we're going." I leaned out past him to look further down the tunnel. It didn't seem to have an end in sight, so perhaps this doorway would take us to our destination after all. Julian tugged until the door was opened and waved me inside. "After you."

Not wanting to appear scared, I discretely leaned my head in to see if I could tell what was waiting for me. It appeared to be another large room, hollowed out of the massive rock mountain. More torches lit the area and I could see several bunk beds on one side with a small stone table on the other. And sitting around it were all of my friends. Everyone except for Brendan.

"Where is he?" I demanded again.

"He is safe for now. It will all depend on you." I was tired of his cryptic words.

"I don't know what you're talking about!"

"You will. Now, please join your friends. I will be back shortly." With that, he moved behind my back and shoved me inside.

I fell to my knees and as the giant stone door banged shut, Daniel rushed to my side. The change must have helped to heal most of his injuries too, although I could see that his right eye was still a little bit swollen.

"Are you okay?" He asked.

I nodded my head and pushed up to my feet. We moved to the far side of the room where Kain and Carissa sat side by side on a stone bench. My heart dropped a bit when I saw her curled up against him, practically sitting in his lap. Kain's left arm draped over her shoulder and his head rested against the top of hers. He made no attempt to acknowledge my presence and that hurt more than anything else.

Daniel and I sat down across from them on an identical bench. We all wore silk robes with Carissa and me in short ones and Daniel and Kain in the version similar to what Julian had on. No one spoke. Although the silence was beyond uncomfortable, I certainly didn't know what to say. This was all my fault and I would rather suffer in silence than have my friends yell at me.

"So now what do we do?" Daniel finally asked. I didn't raise my head to see that he was looking at me and not Kain. Why I was suddenly the one in charge completely dumbfounded me. Wasn't it apparent that I was incapable of such responsibilities?

"Do you know what they might want?" Carissa glanced up at Kain and asked.

He shrugged. "I have no idea, although I think that we should come up with some kind of plan to get out of here."

"Does anyone know where we are?" asked Daniel.

"In a cave," Carissa replied dead pan.

"I'm guessing we're in Virginia," Kain said, ignoring her response. "I've heard about these systems of underwater caverns, but I don't think very many humans have been able to explore them before." We sat there and thought about that for a while until Daniel interrupted the silence again.

"So how do we get out?"

"I don't know," Kain sighed.

"I have an idea," I said, suddenly feeling hopeful again.

EIGHTEEN

"That's your plan?" Carissa exclaimed. "Control them all and waltz out of here?" She was standing now and pacing back and forth between Kain and the table. One hand on her slender hip, the other ran furiously through her hair.

"Carissa..." he pleaded, reaching for her arm. She jerked away from him and turned so that she could face us both.

"No! This is absurd! First we drive across the country to help out someone who did nothing but break your heart, then we get kidnapped trying to stop her from getting killed, and now you want me to follow her insane idea that she can just mesmerize them all and set us free? Why do you continue to be so blind, Kain?"

"I'm not blind, Carissa. Not anymore." Something squeezed my heart with those bitter words. Tears began to blur my vision, but I pushed them away, determined not to let them get the best of me.

Kain stood and pointed to me while speaking to Carissa. "She has a plan and she can do it."

Shocked, I had to ask. "I can?"

He turned to face me. "Yes. I saw you at the bridge. You took control of those selkies and stopped them from beating me to death." He walked toward Carissa and grabbed both of her hands in his. "You didn't see it, but she has the power. And right now we don't have a better plan."

Carissa gazed up into his eyes, although with her height, she didn't have far to look. They glistened with tears and dread, but the way she looked at Kain softened her anger. "You think this is what we need to do?"

"I do." He pulled her into an embrace but not before giving her a quick kiss on the lips.

I flinched without any type of effort to stop myself. Averting my eyes to the floor, I felt Daniel's hand rest on my clenched ones. He squeezed tightly and I shut my eyes to stop the tears. I shouldn't care. I should be happy for Kain. And even for Carissa who had been nothing but a friend to me. But still, the sight of him kissing another girl only invoked feelings of jealousy and rejection. Perhaps this is the way Kain had always felt about Brendan and me. And if that was the case, I was sorrier than I would ever be able to apologize for.

The door to our prison creaked open, sending shards of light into the shadowed crevasses. Kain and Carissa detached themselves as Daniel and I stood up to move next to them. I hoped that they were ready for all of us, but was sadly disappointed when Julian walked in the door and pointed at me.

"Come with me, Eviana."

"What about the rest of them?"

"They will join us shortly."

Daniel squeezed my arms. "Don't go with him," he whispered into my ear.

"She will be perfectly safe," Julian replied, apparently capable of hearing private conversations. Kain stepped ahead of me, effectively blocking my view of the selkie.

"What do you want with her?" he asked.

Julian stared at Kain for a moment. Then his gaze slid over to Carissa and back to me. The corner of his mouth turned up and Kain straightened his shoulders, puffing up for the fight. "My master wants to speak with her." When none of us moved, Julian continued. "You have my word that he is only going to speak with her."

"Your word doesn't hold much stake with us," Kain chided.

"No, but it means something to her." He was pointing at me again.

At once, all eyes were on me but I continued to stare at Julian. He hadn't seemed cruel when we had our conversation not too long ago and there was something about him that made me want to believe him. It wasn't trust, exactly. It was more of a mutual respect.

"I'll be okay," I promised while moving away from my friends and toward the door. Pulling down the back of my short robe, I walked through the opening before turning to look at my friend's faces. "Just sit tight and I'll see you soon."

Daniel shuddered with emotion, terror filled Carissa's eyes, and Kain stood as still as a statue watching me leave them behind.

I followed Julian down the tunnel once he closed, and locked, the door behind him. We didn't speak but somehow I didn't have anything to say. I figured that I needed to save my questions for whomever it was that I was going to see now.

After another hundred yards or so, the tunnel lightened and we entered a second large cavern. Unlike the entrance into the pool, this one had been manipulated to accommodate a number of guests. It was almost like a grand ballroom, with hanging candelabras and archways breaking up the open expanse of the space. The center was filled with large pieces of rock, artfully placed together to create a tiled floor. Along the edges, humans, selkies, and other mermaids watched in silence as we passed by. It reminded me of Jeremiah's home and I instantly got chills down the back of my neck. I feared that I was witnessing another sample of what I would one day be able to do; control my own army.

We made our way to the opposite side, where several thrones were placed. There were three of them, one in the middle and one on each side but slightly behind. The two on the sides were filled with one male and one female mermaid. I had never seen them before even though I frantically searched my brain for some memory of their faces.

It wasn't until I noticed the man standing up next to the largest throne that my fear finally grasped every last nerve. I would never forget those eyes. He spread his arms out wide, gesturing for me to come closer.

"Eviana Dumahl. It is such a pleasure to see you again. Welcome to my abode."

"Master Sutherland." Lucian Sutherland, the man from Cotillion and the one leading the charge to reinstate the Legacy stood ahead of me as pompous and confident as he was before. It is typical to bow slightly out of respect to other clan leaders, but I couldn't bring myself to do it.

Apparently, Lucian didn't mind my lack of etiquette. Instead he hustled up beside me and gave me a hug like we were best friends reuniting after several years. I pulled away and looked at him in disgust.

"Why are we here?" I asked forcefully.

"Well, you are here because I need to speak with you. The others are here due to an unforeseen circumstance." He twirled his fingers in the air like an eighteenth century composer. In fact, his outfit kind of reminded me of that era as well, with the long tail on his velvet jacket hanging down past his knees and the white puffy shirt underneath reminiscent of years past.

"I don't have anything to say to you."

"Oh don't be so hasty, dear. You may very much have something to say after I've given you my proposition."

He walked back to his throne but when I tried to follow, Julian grabbed my shoulder and held me in place. Lucian's theatrical display continued as he whirled around in front of his chair, pushing the long coat tails behind him and out of the way so he could sit. Once settled, he waved his hand at someone in the back of the room and I heard another door open followed by some scuffling. Julian's hand tightened on my shoulder once the new guest was visible to us both. It was Brendan.

He was still in bad shape despite being forced through a transition earlier. In his human form, his ribs were sticking out, his cheeks were sunken in, and his skin was pale. The normally tall statuesque figure was gone, replaced instead by a hunched gaunt one. It was heart wrenching to see him like this. Julian allowed me to move toward Brendan, but his two human guards stopped short. They were not going to let me touch him.

"Are you okay?" I whispered to my love.

He tried to smile and for an instance his green eyes lit up the room. "I've been better."

I smiled back and felt the tears spill from my eyes. Lucian clapped loudly and startled us both.

"Ain't love grand?" he asked the room. No one responded except for the two mermaids in the other thrones who snickered in our direction. "Now, Eviana I need you to focus on me." With great reluctance, I turned to face him, wishing that I could hurt him somehow. "Now, it seems as if we have a bit of problem to deal with. You see, I heard that you were able to take control of some of my selkies, and that is something that does not make me happy."

I heard Brendan shift his stance, uncomfortable with what was just revealed. "I don't know what you are talking about," I denied.

"Now don't be coy, little girl. I've heard it from two of my best. You controlled them and I want to know how it felt."

"How it *felt?*"

"Yes. How intoxicating was that power? That total control over another creature." He placed his elbows on his thighs and leaned over. "It's wonderful isn't it?"

"No!" I screamed.

"No?"

"I didn't even know what happened. But once Julian told me, I realized how wrong that was. No one has the right to control another."

Lucian slumped back in his chair like he was bored and played with a piece of his blond ponytail. "Well that sure is a shame. I was hoping this conversation would go in a much different direction."

"What are you talking about?"

"The Legacy, Eviana. For too many years we've been suppressed and forced to live in a world where we are not respected amongst both shifters and humans. The time has come to end those ways." He stood again and waved over two selkies that replaced Brendan's human guards. I recognized the female as one of our original captors.

"What are you doing?" I asked with a shaky voice.

"You'll see," he replied coyly as he nodded toward the selkies. With one quick move, the female jerked Brendan's hands behind his back. Not hesitating for a second, the young male pulled a knife from his belt and plunged it into Brendan's stomach.

"No!" I screamed.

Brendan's face contorted in pain but the female would not let him fall. I watched in slow motion as the male selkie raised his arm again, preparing for another thrust. This time, I felt the power rise in me without even thinking about it. I pushed it out from the center of my core, through my limbs, and past my fingertips. "Stop now!" I commanded.

The room seemed to take in a collective breath as the selkies froze mid-motion before dropping to their knees and giving me the lost puppy look again. All of the humans followed suit, and much to my surprise, there must have been at least thirty of them. Julian seemed to be unaffected although he was shaking his head as if trying to get rid of my command.

I took a brief moment to look back behind me at Lucian who was smiling with the kind of pride a father would have for his daughter. That made me angrier and I knew that we had to get out of here as soon as possible. But could we? Did I have that strength? Now was my chance to test it. I pointed to four humans kneeling along the back wall.

"You. Come here and take these selkies away." I found an older looking female who I hoped would have a strong maternal instinct. "And you help fix this wound."

Immediately, they sprang into action, doing just what I told them to. The selkies didn't fight, and instead left willingly. I watched as several people assisted the female human with Brendan. They carried him out the room as well, although his eyes never left mine the entire way. The green globes didn't seem to represent the pain he was feeling and my stomach dropped when I realized that I had seized control of him too. He'd warned me about this and it was one of the worst feelings in the world to control someone I love like that. As quickly as it appeared, I dropped my newfound power and marched toward Lucian and his arrogant smile.

"Why the angry face my dear?"

"This isn't right! I don't want to have this kind of power over people. No one should!"

He shot to his feet and closed the gap between us in a few strides. "We should! It is our birthright, given to us a long time ago by our creators. Being forced to live like a human is cruel and condescending." Those blue- grey eyes bore into mine. "You just saved your pet's life. Doesn't that mean something to you?"

"He is not my pet! I don't ever want to take over his mind again." I was sobbing now but I didn't care how immature I looked. This was something that I simply could not accept.

"You will when you need him," Lucian stated matter-of-factly.

I shook my head. "No, I won't. I can't."

"You will be leader soon, Eviana. And not only will you join me, but you will also bring along the Matthew clan as well."

This caught me completely off guard. "You people really don't have your facts straight do you? I walked away from all of that. My mother shunned me and Kain hates me. I will never be a part of our families again." I noticed a hint of confusion pass over Lucian's features before he quickly hid it behind his leader facade. "You didn't know that did you? Maybe living in a cave in the middle of the Virginia mountains isn't quite the best way to keep up to date with the world." Suddenly feeling a little more confident, I threw back my shoulders and glared into his cold eyes. "That's right. I mean nothing to them which means that I mean nothing to you."

Without saying a word, Lucian Sutherland turned on his heel and marched back up to his throne. He sat down, resting his head in his hand like he was in deep thought. Julian's arm wrapped around my shoulders and pulled me away, back toward the tunnel that led to my friends. As soon as we turned the corner and were out of sight of everyone else, the adrenaline that flooded my body dissipated and left me trembling. They stabbed Brendan and I'd stolen his mind.

"I will make sure that he is all right," Julian said, surprising me for a moment. "Brendan. I will go and check on him. One of the mermaids is a healer and I am sure that Master Sutherland does not want him to die."

"Thank you," I whispered. I couldn't even muster up the other questions that I wanted to ask. So we walked to the room in silence, with the opening of the stone door being the only sound in the tunnel. I didn't want to face anyone right now. All I wanted to do was curl up into a ball and cry. My world was falling apart, and I feared that I had just ruined our only chance for escape.

NINETEEN

It was almost two days later before we were able to leave the room again. There were chaperoned bathroom breaks and three meals a day, but we had really been trapped. To make things worse, Julian never came by to give me an update on Brendan, and Kain and Carissa's relationship seemed to be growing every day. If it wasn't for Daniel, I think that I would have lost my mind several times over.

I felt so alone right now.

Not knowing what kind of damage I'd inflicted on my relationship with Brendan was killing me. My power had overtaken him. He was used to taking care of me and I loved that about him. But now the tables had turned and I wasn't so sure that he would be a willing participant.

I silently cried myself to sleep every night. I missed my home and my family, and I wished more than ever that I could go back and think things through a little bit more. What if I would have married

Kain and took him up on his offer to allow me to continue seeing Brendan? I still didn't know how that would have actually worked out, but I was pretty sure that none of us would be here right now if I would have just been unselfish and made the right decision for once in my life.

When we were ushered to the great ballroom again, I was surprised to see that most of the humans were gone and more merfolk were in attendance. A part of me smiled knowing Lucian had removed them from my presence. I had been able to break his control over them. Even though he was testing me, I would imagine that he was still hesitant to give me that opportunity again.

The only downside was that we were counting on having their help to assist us in our escape. In one of the few conversations I had with my friends in our holding cell, I revealed that I took over the minds of several selkies and most of the humans. I even went as far to tell them that I appeared to have limited control of my new found power. Their reactions were mixed, from shocked to inspired. Kain's blank expressions left him somewhere in the middle. But regardless, we came up with a plan.

Now that most of our strategy had failed to show up, I was rapidly trying to count the remaining possibilities without being noticed. Twenty mermaids, several of them clan leaders, were now flanking the three thrones. This was not only disturbing because of the number, but also because I was disappointed to see so many following Lucian's insane platform.

There were about ten selkies present and one of them was Brendan. He made very little eye contact with me when we arrived.

Julian stood by his side, offering a hand on his shoulder. Perhaps there was more going on here and Brendan was just playing a role. Maybe he really did want to be by my side. It was the only shred of hope I could grasp on to.

The sound of our shoes clicking along the stones echoed throughout the cavern. After a day being held captive, they finally gave us back our clothes. Freshly cleaned and pressed, not a stain on them. Whatever. It was better than the silken robes. The noise was ominous, like a ticking clock counting down to our demise. The silence when we stopped was even worse. I searched the thrones for Lucian, but he wasn't here yet.

A door slammed along the side wall, sending pulses of sound in chaotic waves around the room. Master Sutherland waltzed in like a king with several more mermaids behind. They appeared to be escorting someone, yet the way they surrounded each other made it hard to see exactly what was going on.

"Eviana, such a pleasure," Lucian said grandly. "I apologize for the delay, but I had to get a few things in order before continuing our discussions."

"I thought we were finished talking," I said.

Lucian walked up to his throne and made another elaborate show of sitting down. Today he donned black leather pants and a blood red silk shirt. His golden hair hung loose around his shoulders so he could artfully brush it out of his face when he needed something to do.

Finally in his seat, he crossed his legs and propped an elbow up on the arm of the throne.

"Oh no. We still have so much more to discuss. In fact, I am surprised that you have not asked for me after your little display of power the other day." I looked behind me at my friends and then to the side of the room at Brendan. They all knew what happened, but there was still a part of me that cringed at my sudden abilities. Seeing my discomfort, Lucian laughed. "Let me guess, they don't want to be around you anymore. Is that correct?"

"No," I pouted.

"Well then, why the gloomy face?" He leaned forward in his chair. "You are about to become the most powerful leader amongst the non-followers. They will all have to obey you." I looked up at him in confusion and then back at my friends to see that they, too, had no idea what he was talking about.

The shuffling of feet from a doorway drew my attention to the side. A mound of people began to drag their prisoner toward the center of the floor and directly in front of me. They dropped their baggage like a piece of trash and quickly moved away to flank my friends and me. Stunned, I looked down at the battered mermaid before me and nearly lost all control.

My mother's tiny frame was broken and bruised. Her normally beautiful thick dark hair hung in mats and was filled with dirt and something else. As I looked more closely, I could see the cuts on her head, leading me to believe that I was seeing blood. Her left arm appeared to be broken and one of her ankles was swollen bad enough that I doubted she could put any weight on it. The long purple sundress had rips and tears throughout, hidden only slightly by the patches of mud and blood. I couldn't make my legs move fast enough.

"Mom!" Bending my knees, I slid down next to her side while trying not to touch her and cause more distress. She turned her head enough for us to see each other. Tears stained her face and that fierce spark that made her who she was seemed to be gone. Her dark eyes were now just that, dark and empty. I rubbed my hand lightly along her cheek. "No, mom. What did they do to you?"

"Eviana..." she whispered, but I couldn't make out much more of the words. "...missed...father...worried...gone." I leaned closer so that we could have our own private conversation.

"I'm here now, mom. Don't worry about me. You and dad don't have to worry about me anymore." Her face blurred because of the tears filling my eyes. I didn't even try to wipe them away since I knew the flow would not stop.

My mother positioned herself so that she could see more of me. Her face was ripe with pain, but not as a reflection of the physical kind. This pain was much deeper than that.

"No...your father...gone." She was shaking her head but I still didn't understand. "Killed," she breathed.

"What?" My hand stopped soothing her and I jerked my gaze to Lucian. "Where is my father?" I demanded, trying to sound stronger than I felt right now.

Lucian shrugged his shoulders and then pushed to his feet. "He wouldn't let your mother go without a fight."

"Where. Is. He?" I ordered between clenched teeth.

"In California."

"Alive?"

"Not anymore."

In my mind, I watched myself leap over my mother and wrap my hands around Lucian's neck, squeezing so that he wouldn't speak ever again. I beat him until I couldn't move anymore, taking out all of my pain on the man that killed my father.

But what I did instead was much more mature than I would have ever anticipated. Lucian wanted something and if it would get my mother and my friends out of here alive, than I needed to bargain with him. There was a reason that my mother wasn't dead yet.

Standing to face my adversary, I heard Daniel and Carissa crying behind me. I didn't look at them. I would grieve for my father later. "What do you want?" I asked softly.

"I want your clan to join me. The Dumahls and the Matthews will secure enough of a force to make the Council finally listen. They will have to reinstate the Legacy." I shook my head.

"You still don't get it, do you? I am not a part of my clan anymore. I have no authority! I don't even exist in their eyes!"

"You've only been shunned by your leader. Once she is gone the problem is solved." Panic seared through me. What was he going to do?

"I...I can't take leadership from her. It doesn't work that way. She was chosen."

Lucian snapped his fingers and someone instantly grabbed my arms and pinned them behind me. I struggled to break free, but their grip was too strong. My friends were also contained by another group of selkies. There was nothing that we could do now except watch what was coming next.

Lucian sauntered over to my mother who had pulled herself up to her knees to look at her enemy. She turned sideways and it allowed me to see that she was clearly being as defiant as she could in this position. Her chin thrust forward and her shoulders were back, taking one last stance. When Lucian reached her, he brushed a piece of hair behind her ear in a very personal gesture. She allowed it, but I saw her swallow hard.

"Such a waste, Marguerite. Such a waste. You should have accepted my offer." He continued to caress her cheek like a lost lover.

"She will never join you," she said.

"We will see," he replied just before reaching out with inhuman speed and snapping her neck.

"Mom!" I screamed.

The bile in my stomach rose up into my throat. At that moment it seemed as if I was in a dream. Everything moved in slow motion. I nearly ripped my arms out of their sockets from pulling so hard against my captor while the sickening crunch of my mother's bones echoed throughout the cavern. Her lifeless body slumped to the floor for the last time. Lucian followed her down to the ground but I didn't know why. A moment later, he stood, holding her shield in his hand.

He walked toward me as I continued to struggle. I didn't want this. My mother was the leader, not me. I was a selfish runaway child who did not have the knowledge to lead my clan. I could never be like her. And the only two people who could have prepared me for this were now dead. "Stay away from me!"

"Eviana, it is time for you to make a choice. Lead your clan and his and do what is right." He nodded behind me toward Kain, implying that we came as two for the price of one. "This shield is meant for you. Wear it and own it." His hand shot out and the broach flew through the air in my direction. There was nowhere for me to go.

When the shield landed against my chest, I slammed back against the selkie holding me. The golden double wave that represented our clan began to glow. Air rushed out of my lungs and every part of my body tingled. The hair around my face began to fly around in a silent breeze like the naiad's watery tendrils in the mountain lake. Closing my eyes, I tried to focus on that power. The shield had chosen me and I would contemplate the reasons why later. For now, I had to tap into this source and use it to get us out of here. Vaguely, in the background, I could hear Lucian cheering.

"Do you see that?" he asked the crowd. "This is her destiny. It's just marvelous." His sing-song voice almost made me break my concentration. However, the magic coursing through me right now reminded me to focus.

"Kain?" I whispered.

"I'm here," he said right next to me, apparently not being assessed as a threat any longer.

"It's time."

With that, I threw out my hands and opened my eyes, staring at Lucian. The pounding of my heart was almost as loud as the sharp gasps and exclamations from the merfolk watching me pull every selkie and human around under my command. Doors began to open and close throughout the room as more and more humans emerged. Their faces were blank and as they got within a few feet of me, every single one dropped to the ground on their knees. In just a couple of minutes, I was surrounded by three dozen people.

Lucian's expression was weary. He had suspected that I could do this, but I guessed he still wasn't sure if I was on his side or not. "How impressive, Eviana," his voice slightly shaky. "This is why I need you."

"You don't get to make that choice," I said.

A bit of his arrogance appeared again. "You can't control me too."

"I don't need to control you," I said. With a mental shout to those surrounding me, I commanded them to attack Lucian and his allies. I sent in the humans first. Not because they were cannon fodder, but because I wanted the selkies with me. For some twisted reason, I trusted Julian to get us out of here.

The ensuing sounds of hand to hand combat filled the room, as the echoes reverberated off the walls. With another mental push, I pulled all of the selkies into a circular formation around us. Brendan limped up along the side of them but didn't try to come any closer. I swallowed a ball of regret knowing that we would have to talk about this later.

"We have to get out of here!" I demanded. "You five lead the way, the rest follow behind."

We started to move back toward the tunnel that should take us to the underwater cave. Julian headed of the group, not once hesitating over his orders. I looked back at my mother's body lying on the cave floor. I wanted so badly to take her with us, but I knew it could potentially mean the difference between life and death. Not only had I turned Lucian down, but I had captured his army. He would not let that slide.

"Eviana!" Lucian yelled at me while single handedly fighting off four different humans. "You have made a huge mistake! This is not over!"

I shuddered at his threat knowing full well that he planned on coming after us again. I didn't think that the humans could kill him and I also didn't know how long my hold over them would last once I was gone. In fact, I could already feel him pushing against my mind in an attempt to win back control of his subjects.

We ran toward the tunnel faster than I'd ever run before. Brendan was directly in front of me now, and I noticed that he tripped and stumbled much more often than the rest of us. He still wasn't healed completely but my command of his mind had overpowered his body's resistance to its injuries.

When we got to the pool I immediately told everyone to change. The swim was too long for human lungs. Julian ran into a side cavern and before I could call him back, he came out with his arms full of seal skins. It was weird, but at this moment weird would work.

Daniel, Carissa, Kain, and I began to strip off our clothes. My three friends dove into the water together in order to encourage their transition. The ten or so selkies that were still by our side also slipped into their skins and plunged into the pool. Julian and I were the last two on shore.

"Your hold is slipping," he warned.

"I know. I can feel it." Lucian's presence in my mind seemed to suffocate me, and one by one, I could feel my control drop away from individual humans. It was like someone cut the cord from my power to theirs. "How long do we have?" I asked Julian.

"A few minutes at most." He put his arm around my waist and pulled me toward the end of the rock outcropping. "We have to go now."

I didn't get a chance to agree. He pushed me in the water and practically landed on top of me a few seconds later. Even though I was scared, my bones fused with an ease more akin to how the selkies change. I had never had a transition happen so smoothly and when I was admiring my new painless tail, I also noticed something golden reflecting on my waist. The clan shield had made its way to me again. I had forgotten about that when I threw off all of my clothes, but just like Kain had mentioned a while ago, it seemed to want to be attached.

Julian grunted at me under the water. When I grabbed one last breath, I noticed a few humans emerge from the darkness. Lucian had control of them now and we had definitely overstayed our welcome. I dove down to the opening of our escape route with Julian right behind me. Waiting there was my selkie; my Brendan. I smiled for the first time in several days at the sight of him. He blew a few bubbles in my direction before disappearing head first into the tunnel.

The three of us moved so quickly that the sediment from the bottom of the cave created mini vortexes and erased any visibility. The tunnel seemed to go on forever and I had a brief moment wondering if we had gone into the right one. Lucian and his group made the underwater labyrinth suitable for their own needs, so who was to say that there weren't multiple entrances and exits.

That thought had me pushing Brendan, both mentally and physically to move faster. Until we were free of this area, we weren't safe. A few moments later we arrived at the opening. Brendan and Julian shot to the surface, but something in the distance distracted me. I couldn't be sure, but it looked like the water shimmered and the spot was moving closer.

Curiosity got the best of me and I used a couple of powerful kicks to get a better look. The quivering particles reached out toward me and wrapped around my back. It reminded me of a couple of octopi arms and they seemed to be just as strong. I was pulled toward the far side of the pool where the river became shallower and the rocks created a dam to hold back the waterfall's flow.

Struggling to break free of this thing, I was able to breach the surface and call for help. I didn't know who would hear me, but someone had to be nearby. Once I filled my lungs, I looked back underneath the surface to see a pair of watery human arms wrapped tightly around my waist. Following the arms, I searched for a face and almost screamed when one appeared a few inches in front of me.

TWENTY

His pointy teeth and oblong head reminded me of his true nature. "Abhainn!" I screamed underwater. We surfaced together and I immediately pushed him off of me. "What are you doing? Let me go!"

"Eviana, calm down." He moved away from me and raised his translucent hands. "I'm here to help."

"Help? How did you get here?" I looked around the perimeter of the pool and was delighted to see my friends and the selkies emerging from the water and changing forms.

"Let's just say that I can be very persuasive," Abhainn continued.

"Huh?"

"Apparently nixies enjoy making bargains. It only took a few warm bodies to convince them to let me go." His lips curved up into a sinful grin sending chills through my spine.

"I don't want to know," I said wholeheartedly.

"Aye, perhaps some other time then. But for now, ye need to get out of this water."

With one kick, I pushed myself onto the rocky beach and was again surprised that my legs almost instantly returned to me. It was like I only had to think *change* and I did. Maybe it was because of my new position, but regardless, I was very much liking this new me.

"Mistress Dumahl?" Abhainn asked while staring at the shield still attached to my hip. He looked at me with immense curiosity.

"I'll have to explain later." Right now, I couldn't talk about it without grieving for what I'd just lost.

"Eviana, they're coming!" Julian yelled from the far side of the pool. I watched the water's surface, waiting for heads to emerge but no one came.

"There," Abhainn pointed toward the top of the waterfall with an enormous smile.

Suspicious, I followed his lead and turned my head up to the colossal rock outcropping. The water flowed faster and the pounding at the bottom grew exponentially louder. When a tidal wave came barreling over the top of the falls, I watched in fascination as the water flowed out and away from the river and defied gravity.

Two, three, and then at least several more tendrils spilled from the wave and spiraled out toward us. As they came closer to the ground, I saw the outline of a horse's head. First the snout pushed through the curvature of the wave, followed by the top of its head and then finally a neck. When the figures became more prominent, they also started to fill in.

The largest tendril produced the most beautiful black horse I had ever seen in my life. His feet were covered with long hair, making them look like massive stones. Every muscle protruded from his body, highlighting the creature's magnificent curves.

Each horse ran out of the water and onto the rocky shore, dripping and shaking while calling to one another. Aside from the black one, the rest were all pure white and by the time the wave subsided, there were seven horses standing in front of us.

The black one shook his long mane and reared up on his hind legs. The rest of them followed suit, leaving me in awe at their intricate dance. I turned to face Abhainn who remained floating above the water.

"What are they?" I breathed.

"Kelpies."

"Kelpies? They're real?" I gasped. In response, Abhainn raised an eyebrow and gestured to the herd of horses positioned amongst my friends. Of course they were real. "Where did they come from?"

The black one, who appeared to be their leader, trotted over to me. He was at least eight feet tall and I couldn't resist the urge to rub my fingers over his snout. Lowering his head with permission, I rubbed the long lines of face. The fur reminded me of Brendan's seal skin sending a familiar calm throughout my body. His dark black eyes moved back and forth, keeping watch both over me and his herd.

"I brought them," Abhainn continued. I looked at him in confusion. "I figured that ye might need the extra legs. They will help get ye out of the forest much faster." The horse nickered and bobbed his head up and down in agreement.

"I...I don't know what to say." Not only had Abhainn found a way to bargain for his own life, but he had conjured an escape plan for us as well.

"Consider our debts even at this point." He drifted closer toward the center of the pool and began to sink into the dark depths of the water.

"Where are you going?" I called after him. "Will I see you again?" There was a part of me that would miss the unusual water sprite.

"Aye, lassie. We will see each other again." And with that, he disappeared from sight.

The stallion pushed his head into my shoulder, encouraging me to move. The rest of the kelpies stomped their feet on the ground in a sign of restlessness. None of us had mounted the horses, but when merfolk heads began breaking through the water's surface, we didn't hesitate.

"Eviana!" Lucian screamed.

"Come on," I yelled while reaching toward Daniel. In pairs, we all jumped on the kelpies and began riding away. We were the last to leave the waterfall, and when I looked back at Lucian, his face was twisted in rage and disgust. I knew that this wasn't the last that I would see of him. He would come after me and my clan with a vengeance. The only thing that I could do now was get back home and prepare.

I kicked my heels into the side of the kelpie and grasp the thick black hair of his mane. Daniel's arms wrapped so tightly around my stomach, I could barely breathe. We didn't look back again as we galloped down the river's edge. Each kelpie seemed to float effortlessly over the water as though they were still a part of it. We dodged around low hanging branches and jumped giant boulders. I had never been on a horse before, and if I hadn't been running for my life, I might have had a chance to enjoy how truly magical it was.

The moonlight reflected off the water and the white kelpies making them seem like they were glowing. Kain and Carissa were on the horse directly beside us. She was leaning against his back with her eyes closed, giving total trust to Kain and their kelpie. I remembered letting Brendan take care of me like that.

After tonight, everything was going to change. Would Brendan forgive me for taking control of him? Would my clan accept me as their new leader after everything I did? I knew this was a turning point for me. Today was the day that I had to grow up. No more selfishness. No more tantrums. I had to face the music, so to speak, and I have to admit that I was more than a little bit scared.

We rode down the river for thirty minutes before the kelpies stopped. The forest was began to disappear and it seemed as though this was as far as the water horses were willing to go to avoid being discovered. After I dismounted, Julian and Brendan made their way to my side.

"We can go to Keith's to get some clothes," Julian said.

"Who's Keith?"

"One of the selkies. He lives a few miles up the road and he's already on his way there for a car. We all need clothing."

It was true that every single one of us was naked, leaving our belongings behind at the base of the waterfall. Hopefully Lucian and his crew would take care of that so as to not create any suspicion about missing human swimmers.

I nodded my head in thanks and looked past him at Brendan. He smiled weakly at me and that was invitation enough. In two steps, I closed the distance between us and threw my arms around his waist. With my head buried in his chest, I began to cry. Brendan wrapped one arm around my back and the other rested on my head. He kissed the top of my hair and held me for what felt like hours.

When he gently pushed me away, I looked up into his green eyes and saw the one thing that I feared most. Doubt. Something had changed between us and I didn't know if I would be able to fix it.

"Brendan, I am so sorry for what I did to you," I stammered.

He immediately looked down to the ground and let go of my arms. I noticed that Daniel and Julian left, presumably to give us some space. And although this was not really the time or the place to have that ultimate discussion, some things needed to be said right now.

Brendan sighed and ran a hand through his dark hair. I couldn't help but notice how the movement of his muscles was captured in the moonlight, or the way the slight stubble on his face made him look a few years older. Or the way that he would no longer make eye contact with me. My heart began to break into pieces.

"Eviana," he breathed. "I love you. I will always love you…"

"But…" I cut in with desperation.

"But things have changed. You've changed."

"Brendan, no." I took a step closer to him and attempted to reach out for his hand. He flinched and pulled away from me. It was a very slight movement, but it was still there. "I can't lose you too," I managed to get out. "Not now. Please."

Both of my parents were dead, I'd become a clan leader less than an hour ago, and now the only person in my life that could help me get through all of this was trying to push me away. I felt the numbness taking over my legs and tried to keep myself standing.

Brendan finally looked up at me and I could see that his eyes were shimmering with fresh tears. "I just need some time to think," he said.

"What is there to think about?" I shrieked. "We love each other! We're meant to be with each other. I…I don't understand what else there is to think about!" I was sobbing so hard that most of the words were muffled.

"Evs, please don't cry," he begged. All I could do was huff. I turned my back to him and looked out over the waning river. What kind of reaction did he expect me to have? He wanted to "think" about our relationship which really meant that we were on track toward a breakup. He was doing this right when I needed him the most. I knew that he'd be upset, but I was hoping we could work through it.

"I won't do it again," I whispered.

"What?"

I twisted my head back so that I could see him again. "I won't ever control you again. I swear it!"

"Oh, Evs." He came closer and hugged me against him. "It's not just that." I tried to pull away to question him, but he held me still. "You are a leader now. Everything is going to change. Everyone around you will change. There won't be room for me anymore."

"How can you say that?"

"Because it's true. You will not be allowed to associate with me any longer." He paused and took a deep breath. "They will want you to marry Kain."

I pushed away from him so hard that I almost stumbled to the ground. The sadness and desperation were apparent on his face and as he wiped his eyes, the words began to soak into my bones. Marry Kain? We'd already been through that.

"I will dictate who I can and cannot see." When he looked at me with pity, I continued. "If I truly am the new leader, I can do as I please. Besides, Kain won't marry me anyway. I've already messed that up well beyond repair. I don't even know if we will be able to work together. He hates me right now."

Brendan smiled although it seemed forced. "He doesn't hate you." His tone was almost disappointed but I didn't understand why.

"Well it doesn't matter because I don't want to be with him. I want to be with *you*."

He shook his head. "I don't know…"

"Brendan! I love you. I need you! Why isn't that enough?" The tears were back and this time my legs did give out. I collapsed to my knees, sobbing uncontrollably. My world was falling apart around me and I honestly didn't know how I would survive. He was my best friend. I knew that his presence by my side would cause some uproar, but I didn't care. I was in charge of one of the most powerful clans. Soon, I would be responsible for making all kinds of decisions, so why did this one have to be out of my control? It wasn't fair.

I felt Brendan's long, lean arms pull me against him as he knelt down beside me. He rubbed his hand in circles along my back while I continued to cry, staying silent for a very long time. When he finally spoke, the last of my heart shattered in pain. "I just need some time away from you to sort this out, okay?"

What was I supposed to say? Did I want him to leave me? Absolutely not. I couldn't imagine my life going on without him. Did I want him to take some time? I guess if it gave me a chance to prove that we could make this work, then that was my only option. It would be hard and painful but if it brought him back to my side where he belonged, then I was willing to give him his space.

With his impeccable timing, Julian walked through the tree line and called to us. "They're here." I could feel Brendan nod in acknowledgement but I didn't want to look at him right now. I couldn't.

We stood and joined the rest of the group without saying another word to each other. He stayed next to me, but it felt like an invisible barrier had been erected around each of us. I was heartbroken over his words, devastated that my parents were gone, and somewhat embarrassed that everyone seemed to sense what was happening with my relationship.

Daniel discretely moved to my side and squeezed my hand, causing me to lose all control again. I squeezed back and looked out at the road where a large multi-passenger van had just pulled off the side. We all started to walk in that direction in silence. Keith, at least I think it was him, began passing out bath towels as we got closer to the van.

If I was feeling anything at that moment, I would have thanked him for being considerate, but I couldn't muster the strength.

Since I was the last one to climb into the van, I noticed there was only one seat left. I sat down next to Kain and Carissa, giving Brendan his space in the seat behind us. Apparently some of the selkies had either left already or walked to Keith's initially, because there were only three of them now in the van. As we pulled away from the forest, I could feel Kain's eyes on me. I couldn't look at him right now either, so I turned and watched the scenery out the side window.

The trees flew by and soon gave way to manicured lawns and residential houses. I still didn't know exactly where we were, but I really didn't care right now. I couldn't feel anything. Didn't want to.

When we arrived at Keith's house, Julian ushered us inside and kind of took charge. It was obvious to everyone that I had mentally checked out back at the forest, and for the most part they left me alone. Dawn was rising before Julian volunteered to take the five of us back to the beach and our hotel.

We piled in the van once more, and although Brendan came along, he sat in the passenger seat which left me in the rear one. Daniel sat next to me, but I rested my head on the back of the seat and closed my eyes. The gravity of the night's events was drowning me right now. I focused on my breathing which helped me swallow the tears.

Every once and a while I would listen to the conversations between Kain and Carissa or Brendan and Julian. But if someone asked me to repeat them, I wouldn't have been able to. Background noise. That's all they were.

PROMISES

It was well after lunch before we pulled into the visitor's center at the Bay Bridge. Surprisingly, Brendan's car was still there and without saying a word to anyone, he jumped out of the van to drive himself to the hotel. Something about that burned in me and I was forced to lie down in the back seat so that no one would see my anguish. Daniel, understanding that I was not going to be good company, moved up front with Julian for the remainder of the ride. I was exhausted, in every sense of the word.

So much of me wanted to sleep and pretend that all of this was a dream. I would wake up with Brendan by my side in our bed at the hotel. He would brush the hair out of my face and make fun of me for drooling in my sleep. We would pretend to fight, make up in bed, and then swim in the ocean together for the rest of the day. That was the dream I had always wanted. The dream that I'd left my family for. The dream that I'd hurt Kain over. And now I feared that it was a dream I could no longer have. I didn't want anything else. Nothing else in this world mattered if I couldn't have Brendan. Nothing.

We finally made it to the hotel and I went about my tasks in a daze. Julian waited outside while Brendan and I packed up our meager belongings and set them by the door. At some point, Brendan left to check out, giving me a moment to grieve over the loss of the life I so briefly got to enjoy.

Holding a small framed picture of the two of us at sunset, I couldn't help but smile. I don't think that I was smiling at the memory, but I was laughing at the situation. Everything I ran away from had come back to haunt me. I avoided marrying Kain, I never wanted to lead my clan, and most importantly, I never wanted to have a life that didn't include Brendan. In just a few days, my world had disintegrated. Maybe Brendan was right. Maybe things were going to be different now.

The door to our room bounced open against the wall causing me to jump. "Sorry," Brendan said. He saw me sitting on the edge of the bed and sat down by my side. "That was a good night." I looked at him to see that he was referring to the picture in my hand.

"Yeah?"

"Yeah. Remember all of the rays we saw?" I smiled and shoved the photograph into his hand.

"You keep this. To remember." My voice was shaky but I managed to go on. "You remember how great it is when we are together. No one can ever take that away from us, Brendan. No one."

"I'm not going back to California right now," he suddenly blurted out.

"What?" The giant lump in my throat returned and it took everything I had to swallow it back down.

"I'm going with Julian for a while."

I paused, trying to get a handle on my emotions. "And where is that?"

"Seattle."

"Oh," I whispered. Time. *He needed time* I told myself. It was the only way I could get him back. "For how long?"

"I don't know," he said quietly.

"Oh."

He let out a breath and brushed his fingers over the photograph. "I'll try not to be too long."

In the most grown up thing I'd ever done in my life I said, "Take all of the time you need. I will be here, waiting for you when you're ready to come back."

What I really wanted to do was kick and scream and beg for him to stay by my side. I couldn't live without him, therefore I didn't care what he wanted as long as he stayed. But I had to grow up now.

He rested his hand on my thigh, sending a different kind of chill through me. "Thank you, Evs."

With that, he stood and walked out the door, not once looking back over his shoulder.

Twenty One

I stayed in the room long enough to be certain that Brendan and Julian had left. I didn't want to face my friends, but it was inevitable. We were all driving back to California together. Two days in the car would mean that at some point I would need to speak to them. Unfortunately, it happened a little sooner than I expected.

"Can I come in?" Kain asked. He stood in the doorway and I hadn't yet moved from my perch at the edge of the bed. It may have been five minutes, twenty minutes, or an hour. I didn't know how long I'd been sitting there.

"Sure," I choked out. "Are you guys all ready?" Wiping my eyes and nose, I tried to put on a mature face. He sat down next to me.

"Yeah, we're ready when you are." After a long pause he asked, "Brendan's not coming?" I shook my head, afraid that speaking would break open the floodgates. "I'm sorry," he said solemnly.

I stared at him. He appeared sincere, but for the life of me I had no idea why this guy was still being nice to me. Wasn't it obvious by now that I screwed up every relationship in my life? That I was incapable of keeping friends, lovers, or family members close to me? Wasn't it obvious that I was a horrible person?

"So, Julian had a few things to discuss while you were packing," Kain continued.

"Julian?"

"Yes. He seems to think that we are going to need his help for the upcoming war."

"War?" I questioned. "What war?"

"The one that you incited against Lucian?" I looked at him again. "He's going to come after us all, Eviana. You are just as strong if not more powerful than he is and now that he's seen that, he will not stop until you are gone. And along with the Dumahls come the Matthews so he'll be coming after both of us."

This was just too much right now.

"Kain…I can't." Shaking my head back and forth I finally pushed my face into my hands. "I just can't deal with this right now."

"You don't have a choice, Eviana. You are the leader now, whether you like it or not. With that comes a responsibility for the safety and security of your people. Your personal issues no longer take precedence."

"I understand that but…"

"No! You don't get to sulk. You don't get to grieve for your loss. Your time is over. A war is coming and we need to prepare. *You* need to prepare, Eviana. You need to act like the leader everyone knew that you were meant to be." He grabbed the shield on my chest and pulled it far enough away that I could look down and see it. "This means that you were destined, Eviana. Your mother was an amazing leader but now it's your time. People are counting on you. I'm counting on you."

That comment caught my attention. "What do you mean?"

"Your mother and I had all but joined our two families together after you left." I cringed at the hidden meaning behind those words. "We presented a united front and I think it's in all our interest if we continue to do so." He finally dropped the shield but picked up my hand instead. "You and I are going to have to work closely together in order to keep Lucian away and build trust amongst our clan members. We are young and not everyone will think that we're up for the job. But together we are strong. We can prove to them that we are worth following and that we will protect our people."

I looked into his blue eyes and smiled wistfully. He had such faith in me. Even after I'd proven that his loyalties were misplaced time and time again, he was still standing by my side. I'd literally left him at the altar but yet he came to help me when I asked. I didn't deserve this kind of treatment from anyone, but most of all from him.

I squeezed his hand. "Why are you so good to me?"

He sighed and looked down at his feet. "Because I love you, Eviana." Before I could reply, he continued. "It might be a different kind of love now, but I still care. I always will." He reached up and wiped away a tear falling down my cheek. We stared at each other for a moment.

"I'm so sorry for what I did to you."

"I'll live," he replied with a crooked grin.

"No, it wasn't right. I didn't handle things right. I'm sorry. You deserve so much more." He huffed and tried to pull his hand away, but I held tight. "Carissa is good. She's good for you," I finally said.

He quickly turned his head away. "It's not like that with her."

"But maybe it can be. And you deserve it, Kain. You deserve to be happy." He smiled and focused ot the floor. It was incredibly uncomfortable to have this conversation with each other, but it needed to be said. He needed to know how important he was to me and how much better off he'd be without me consuming his heart.

"We should go. It's going to be a long trip." He stood and offered me a hand up. I accepted and when I was off the bed, he pulled me into an unexpected hug. "I'm so sorry about your parents," he breathed into my ear.

Suddenly, it dawned on me. I didn't get to be selfish about the death of my parents or the loss of the love of my life because he'd never had that opportunity either. His father died, he became clan leader, and I ran away all within a few days of each other. Still, his responsibilities trumped all other situations and he was forced to carry on. Ironically I was now in a nearly identical situation. At least I had Kain by my side to guide me through it.

I pulled back and looked up at him. He smiled down at me with sympathy in his eyes and his wonderful heart on his sleeve. His attractive tanned face and streaked blonde hair only added to the beauty that he possessed inside.

I reached up to touch his cheek, feeling another tear trickle from my eye. He placed his hand on top of mine and held it there, against his face, then briefly closed his eyes. For a moment the whole world felt right. No more pain. No more war. Just the two of us standing here on the precipice of a new beginning. He started to lean toward me and I didn't stop him. I wanted to feel the warmth of his lips on mine again. I needed it right now. I needed someone to love me.

"We have to get...going," Carissa stuttered from the doorway. Her presence filled the room instantly and I could not only see, but feel Kain tense. He jumped away from me and pushed his hands into his pockets. I stood there, not really knowing what to do or say.

"Huh," Carissa said. She hadn't moved any closer but her hands were now on her hips and she was glaring at Kain. "Looks like I got here just in time."

"Carissa...don't," Kain said with a sigh. He started to walk toward her, but she turned on her heel and stomped out of the room. He followed closely behind, calling after her with despair.

And for the second time that day, another guy walked away from me.

I finished packing my meager belongings, opting to leave behind some of the things that Brendan and I bought together. It was too painful to see them and perhaps they would give the next couple better luck. With one last look around the tiny efficiency, I pulled the door shut for the final time.

Daniel quickly grabbed my bags without saying a word. He hauled them to Kain's expensive car and loaded up the trunk. Carissa was already in the passenger seat, staring ahead and forcing herself to appear indifferent. I could tell that she was upset, and that was just one more person that I now owed an apology too.

It was going to be a nightmare when we got home. I doubted that anyone had heard about my mother yet and my heart dropped when I thought about my sister. She would be devastated. And she would blame me. In all honesty, she had every right to. It was my decision to run away that ultimately led to the death of our parents and my ascension to clan leader, two things that she would have never wanted to happen.

I sighed and looked up at the sky. The warm salty air wrapped me in its embrace, soothing me for just a moment. I recalled meeting the lake naiad and her premonition that I had a lot to learn and my journey would not be long. She was right in saying that I had little time to adjust to my new life. I had absolutely no time at all.

There was a war coming to our people. A war that needed to be handled before the humans suspected anything. All of us would have to fight and some of us would likely die. I was the one making those life and death decisions now. Me and me alone. Kain may say that he'll be there too, but he had his own clan to worry about. And now he also had Carissa.

But I was alone. Brendan was off deciding whether or not he wanted to be with me, which hurt me more than I could ever imagine. He needed his space and his time, but how long could I really wait for him? How long would it be before I stopped hurting? I didn't have the answers right now. Only time would tell how my life was going to go. And right now, my time was running short.

Two car doors slammed shut as Kain and then Daniel crawled inside. The ignition purred while my friends waited for me to join them. With one last deep breath I stepped forward. It was time for me to face my destiny. It was time to go home.

Continue reading for a sneak peak at *Betrayal*, Book Two of The Syrenka Series available now.

ONE

I wanted to punch him in the face.

For at least the hundredth time today, I swung my fist towards his infuriating smirk. He easily dodged it, of course, and proceeded to look down at me like a child. "You're getting closer," he teased.

Throwing my arms down in frustration, I shook my head. "How am I supposed to learn if you won't even let me get a hit in?"

He laughed and resumed a fighter's stance. "How are you supposed to learn if I just stand still and let you pummel me? That's not ever going to happen in the real world. Now, try with your legs."

I rolled my eyes and shifted my feet so that my stronger right leg was in front. Ideally, I'd be having this battle underwater where my legs were not an issue.

"Protect your face," he yelled at me and I lifted my fists up to nose level. I could do this. He'd taught me how to incapacitate my enemies. *Just go for the knee.*

I faked a few smaller kicks, pretending to hesitate. Then, like a ninja, I struck. The underside of my right foot was directly on target and I expected it to land a perfect hit to the side of his left knee. Only it didn't happen.

Out of nowhere, he grabbed my ankle and I was suddenly airborne. The world spun around me once before I landed with a thud on my back, effectively knocking the air from my lungs. I even saw some stars floating by. My training sessions were getting harder every day, and after this debacle, I decided that it was time to quit.

A shadow moved above me and I used my hand to block out the rest of the sun. Looking up at his ominous figure I said, "I'm done."

I heard another laugh rumble through my trainer's chest as he reached down and grabbed my arm. In one swift motion, he pulled me up off the ground.

"You would have broken my knee with that kick, Eviana. I had to stop you." I glared at him. "What?" he continued. "I'm not going to *let* you hurt me. But you did well. I knew that you'd learn eventually."

I jumped towards him as fast as I could, intending to get him in a choke hold. My arms slipped around his neck, but my body kept rolling over him as he bent forward and used my momentum to toss me towards the ground. In less than two seconds, I was on my back again with a forearm pressing against my throat and my pride seeping away into the dirt.

"Ahh!" I screamed in frustration. The annoying grin on his face told me that I would never beat him in a fair fight. Palmer was my cousin, my trainer, and also one of the numerous protectors now living at my house. We'd been practicing for the past two weeks and although I couldn't hurt him yet, Palmer reassured me that I was improving.

Ever since Lucian Sutherland killed my parents a few weeks ago, the security around here increased. As the new clan leader, I wanted all of my people to learn how to fight. No one would be helpless against an attack. There was a war brewing amongst the various merfolk clans, with my family seemingly taking the lead against the uprising. It was not a position I'd ever expected to be in, nor ever wanted. In fact, I ran away from this life for a chance to be with my boyfriend and not be forced into an arranged marriage and clan leadership. But that all fell apart the moment Lucian and his followers attacked me and my friends and pulled me into the center of the merfolk politics I'd always tried to ignore.

"Do you yield?" Palmer asked while pressing a little too hard against my throat. I gave him the most deadly look I could muster and tried to push against his mind. It was futile. Mermaids couldn't control each other like that.

But we could use compulsion on humans. It was what the clans were fighting over now; the right to practice The Legacy and secure our status of god-like creatures in this rapidly evolving world. Controlling humans meant directing the stock market, influencing world politics, and dictating numerous other scenarios that I really hated to think about. Lucian wanted me to join him in his cause to help persuade the Council, our governing body, to allow us to manipulate the minds of lesser species. I had refused his offer and that had cost me everyone that I loved.

Thinking about this made me angry. With my newfound strength, I kicked my legs and aimed for any part of Palmer's body that I could reach. His arm pressed harder against my throat as he scrambled out of the way, barely avoiding a hit to his most precious area.

"Oh, you're in trouble now," he warned. Palmer's grip lightened slightly and his free hand moved towards my ribs. In an instant, he began tickling me so hard that although I tried to resist, I couldn't. Tears spilled out of my eyes and I couldn't catch my breath.

"Stop it! You're going to make me pee my pants," I managed to say in between the giggles.

"That wouldn't be very attractive," a new voice chimed in. Palmer and I sat up instantly and I could feel the heat rising up to my cheeks.

"Good afternoon, Master Matthew," Palmer said after he jumped to his feet. I remained sitting on the ground to give myself a chance to recover and to make sure that I really did have control over my bladder.

"Palmer, you can call me Kain," the new guy said lightly. Kain was almost six feet tall with an athletic body and sun bleached shaggy blonde hair. It was growing out a little bit now, and it seemed as though he didn't quite know what to do with it. He was my age and a clan leader himself. His smile was always friendly but I knew that his dark sunglasses hid disturbingly haunted eyes.

Kain was the fiancé I'd abandoned not long after his father died and he assumed leadership. We had been promised to each other since we were children but I never really had any intentions of marrying him.

My heart had always belonged to Brendan; my selkie. Brendan was a shape shifting seal, and with my abilities to control all selkies, no one thought that we should be together. After the events a few weeks ago, Brendan began to feel the same way and had decided not to return home with me. I hadn't heard much from him since he left and often worried that our relationship was over.

Although my friendship with Kain was still on the rocks due to my actions, we were trying to keep our clans united in the face of war. He was frequently a guest at our house and his budding relationship with Carissa seemed to keep him content. We never spoke about our almost kiss. That was probably for the better, although I would sometimes find myself wondering what would have happened had I chosen a different path. Kain was an amazing guy and quickly becoming a respectable leader. And I couldn't help but realize that Carissa was a lucky girl.

"Sure, Master….um…Kain, sir." Palmer continued stuttering out his words as though he was standing in front of a rock star. "Are you here for practice?" My cousin looked around nervously. "I hope I haven't missed an appointment."

"Oh no. I had a water session this morning and I'm spent," Kain said with a smile. He had a way of making those around him feel at ease with very little effort. It was a really great quality and one I wish that I could master. "I'm actually here to talk to Eviana." Kain looked down at me and I couldn't tell if we were going to have a good or a bad conversation.

I stood and brushed off the sand from my body. My hair pulled against the back of my head, so I retied my ponytail to keep the long blonde pieces from falling in my face again. Trying to be casual and confident I threw back my shoulders and faced my cousin.

"Palmer and I are finished now." Turning back to Kain, I added, "Why don't we go inside so I can get a drink."

He nodded and we began to trek back towards the house. I felt something hit the back of my skull and I spun around to glare at my so-called protector. He was standing there with a huge smile on his face tossing a small pebble up and down in his right hand.

"Remember your training is never over, Eviana." He threw the pebble at me again and I swatted it away. Tipping an invisible hat in my direction, Palmer turned around and jogged off towards the other guys training further down the beach.

"Jerk," I muttered under my breath. Kain laughed.

"That's pretty tame of you."

"Yeah, well…see how grown up I am now? I didn't bother to call him one nasty name that came to mind."

He smiled at me. "I'm impressed." My heart did a little flip-flop. I knew that I had messed things up pretty bad, so any compliment from Kain was encouraging at this point.

We climbed the stairs leading up to the expansive redwood deck my ancestors had built around our house. Just before reaching the top, a petite figure with long dark hair like my mother's leaned over the top of the railing and began waving her arms at us.

"Eviana! Kain! You need to come inside now!"

"We're already on our way, Marisol." My little sister had also been forced to grow up after our parent's death. She and I still didn't get along most days, but over the past few weeks she seemed to realize that putting our differences aside would be the only way we could live together. Plus, I was her legal guardian now so she really didn't have much of a choice.

"Well move faster!" she yelled. "You need to see this!"

I had no idea what she was talking about. Maybe she learned a cool defensive move or maybe her new cat was doing something cute. I didn't really care to be honest. She still blamed me for our parent's deaths and she didn't hide her true feelings about my promotion to clan leader. We had a damaged relationship; that was for sure.

Marisol disappeared inside just as we reached the top. Shaking my head, Kain and I silently continued towards the sliding glass doors that opened up into a large kitchen and dining area. The television was blasting from the adjacent living room where we had been summoned to. Quickly grabbing a bottle of water, I leaned around the counter to see that almost everyone inside was gathered in front of the large flat screen, vying for a spot to see the show. I looked questioningly at Kain, who had waited for me, but his slight shake of the head told me that he didn't know what was going on either.

"Eviana!" Marisol's squeaky voice called again, although this time it was tainted with something I couldn't quite place. Maybe fear or despair and my stomach dropped at her tone.

I pushed my way to the front of the crowd to see what all the fuss was about. One of the local channels was on and the words "Breaking News" kept flashing across the top corner of the screen. Marisol was sobbing and while a female protector tried to soothe her.

"Can someone turn this up?" I asked trying to ignore her sniffling so I could hear what was happening.

The newscaster, a thirty-something year old man with perfectly manicured hair and an award-winning solemn face, began to speak. "I am standing outside of The Wensler Academy where a student has just been arrested for shooting several others earlier in the day. Eighteen-year-old Justin Bernard," he said while reading from his notes, "was detained by police almost an hour ago. Sources say that Mr. Bernard came to school with a loaded pistol and brutally attacked three female students."

Pictures of the injured girls flashed on the screen and I sucked in a panicked breath. "Kristy Smith, Carlee Robinson, and Mia Sarcowski all sustained serious injuries when Justin opened fire on them without warning." The newscaster disappeared and an interview with an eyewitness student filled the screen.

"He kept mumbling the same words over and over. I couldn't understand him but it sounded like 'I must hurt her friends'." The redheaded boy shifted nervously and his eyes darted to and from the camera.

"Do you know whose friends?" asked the reporter. The boy continued shaking his head.

"No. I don't. It's just so weird. Justin wasn't like that. He would never hurt anyone. I…I don't understand…" His attention jerked towards the crowd behind him where Justin and the police had just emerged from the building. The star athlete's hands were cuffed behind his back and two officers were escorting him by the elbows. They hustled him to the car, but not before the reporter stuck the microphone in front of his face.

"Why did you do it, Justin? What was going through your mind?"

I didn't know Justin well, but from what I could see of him right now, there was something very wrong. His pupils were dilated and his lips never stopped moving. He wouldn't answer the reporter's questions and instead stared straight ahead as if in a daze. Just before the police pushed his head into the backseat of the car, the camera man got a close enough shot for me to pick out a few words.

It was only three little words but they sent ice through my veins. How was this possible? What could he mean? None of it made sense to me and when he said "hurt Eviana Dumahl" over and over, the reality of what this could represent suddenly came crashing down.

About the Author

Amber Garr spends her days conducting scientific experiments and wondering if her next door neighbor is secretly a vampire. Born in Pennsylvania, she lives in Florida with her husband and their furry kids. Her childhood imaginary friend was a witch, Halloween is sacred, and she is certain that she has a supernatural sense of smell. She writes both adult and young adult urban fantasies and when not obsessing over the unknown, she can be found dancing, reading, or enjoying a good movie.

Other Titles Now Available

Betrayal – Book Two of The Syrenka Series
Arise - Book Three of The Syrenka Series

Coming Soon

Touching Evil – A Leila Marx Novel

Connect with Amber Garr Online:

www.ambergarr.com
http://ambergarr.blogspot.com
www.facebook.com – Author Page: Amber Garr

2435224R00134

Printed in Great Britain
by Amazon.co.uk, Ltd.,
Marston Gate.